PATRICIA LAKE

moment of madness

D0036868

Harlequin Books

TORONTO • NEW YORK • LOS ANGELES • LONDON
AMSTERDAM • PARIS • SYDNEY • HAMBURG
STOCKHOLM • ATHENS • TOKYO • MILAN

Harlequin Presents first edition May 1983
ISBN 0-373-10593-2

Original hardcover edition published in 1983
by Mills & Boon Limited

"Are you really so blind about men?"

Jase tilted up her face, caressing her jaw with his thumb, forcing her to meet his shadowed golden eyes.

"I've had years of practice," Lexa replied bitterly.

Jase smiled at her, his face tender, and she caught her breath.

"Once you were very sure about love," he said deeply, and she hated him for reminding her. She had offered him everything then, and he had thrown it all back in her face. How dare he mention it now?

"You soon set me straight about that, though," Lexa retorted icily. "Schoolgirl fairy tales, wasn't it?"

"You seem to have got over it nonetheless," Jase said coolly, a faint hint of questioning in his voice.

Lexa felt like laughing. She had never got over him—and she never would.

CHAPTER ONE

THE 'plane taxied slowly to a halt and Lexa peered out of the tiny window, smiling to herself. Home at last, and the sun was actually shining!

The man who had been sitting beside her during the journey watched her with smiling regret as she collected her hand luggage and pulled on her pale linen jacket. Lexa smiled back, friendly yet very slightly cautious. They had chatted together all the way from Switzerland and she could not mistake his interest in her. He was young, French and very self-assured, his dark eyes never leaving her face or her body, their caressing insolence appreciative yet not insulting.

They left the plane together, walking along seemingly endless white corridors to queue at official desks. Lexa's thoughts were far away. She was thinking about the house, the family. Would anybody be here to meet her? She hoped so. It would be such a drag if she had to waste time hiring a car, or fighting for a taxi.

She collected her suitcases, luckily grabbing an empty metal trolley. She had lost sight of Michel, the young Frenchman. She had almost forgotten him.

Slowly she pushed the trolley through customs and suddenly saw her stepbrother, Nick. He was smiling and within seconds he was at her side, kissing her face, hugging her tightly. 'Lexa, it's good to see you—I thought I was going to be late, the traffic is hell as usual.'

'Hello, Nick.' She hugged him back, her eyes bright and happy. It was so good to be home.

Over Nick's shoulder she caught sight of Michel. He was talking to an older man, shaking hands. His eyes met Lexa's and he lifted his hands in expressive regret and farewell.

She smiled and turned back to Nick, her eyes travelling over him affectionately. His dark hair was long and untidy, he was wearing jeans and a short corduroy jacket, his face lean and animated as he talked. He had not changed, which was somehow reassuring after all this time.

'How are you?' she asked seriously, gazing into his light brown eyes.

He smiled. 'Okay, And you?'

'I'm glad to be back at last. Two years is a long time.' A faint shadow of sadness haunted her green eyes.

'Too long,' Nick agreed, taking the trolley from her. 'I missed you.'

Lexa laughed and slid her arm into his as they made their way to the car. 'I missed you too—I missed everyone.' Her mind suddenly crowded with Jase's image. She had missed Jase more than any of the others; she did not know why.

Nick piled her cases into the boot of the waiting white sports car and helped her into the passenger seat. The engine roared into life and they shot off towards the city.

Nick turned his head towards her, his fingers drumming impatiently on the wheel as they stopped at yet another red light.

'You're looking great—did I tell you that?'

'No, I don't think you did.' She pushed a hand through the softness of her blonde curls, her emerald eyes narrowed against the glare of the sun. 'You don't look too bad yourself,' she teased him gently, pleased by his compliment.

The car was moving again. Recognised and re-membered landmarks brought memories flooding back. Yes, he was right. Two years was too long, and now she was back she did not know why she had stayed away.

'How is everybody?' she asked, suddenly longing for news. 'Tell me everything.'

Nick placed a cigarette between his lips, offering her one. She shook her head. He exhaled slowly.

'Rex is the same as ever. The doctors have advised him to take things slower, but he's still working too damned hard. Perhaps you can persuade him to ease up a little, now you're back.'

'You're joking!' Lexa smiled as she thought of her stepfather, his kindness, his lightning temper, his strong forceful personality. She would not be able to persuade him to do anything he did not want to do.

Would he really be pleased to see her, or would she remind him too much of his dead wife, Lexa's mother? He had sounded so sure on the telephone. He wanted her back, he said, but she still felt a tiny niggling of anxiety, of nervousness.

'Well, maybe I am. The redoubtable Mrs Frone has been fighting a losing battle with him ever since he had that heart attack.' Nick flashed her a warm smile. 'She's been baking since early this morning, we're in for something special at dinner, in honour of your homecoming.'

Lexa laughed. Mrs Frone had been Rex's housekeeper for years and years. Stern and formidable, she ruled the house with a rod of iron, though they all knew that she had an impossibly kind heart.

'Is Marny home?' she asked.

'Yes, Jase too—a full house, in fact.'

'Jase?' Lexa's heart turned over.

'He flew in from New York last week—I reckon he

wanted to see Rex. He says he needs some peace, a break from the rat race,' Nick told her casually.

They were out of London now, speeding through the outskirts towards the country, towards the house, towards Jase.

She had not seen Jase for over two years. The last time had been at her mother's funeral. He had been so kind then, so gentle. It hit her just how much she had missed him. She longed to see him again, a yearning so strong it twisted her heart as she sat staring out of the car window at the flat countryside speeding by outside.

'You're very quiet,' Nick remarked, as the silence between them lengthened.

'I'm a little tired.' It was not a lie, but it was not the reason for her silence.

'And worried? he hazarded perceptively.

'Perhaps. I. . . . Rex . . .' she faltered.

'He wants you back. We all want you back, you're part of the family,' he assured her.

'Not really,' she said with a strained smile.

'Yes, really. True, we're not blood relations, but we all love you and it'll be fine, you'll see.'

'Thanks, Nick.' She squeezed his arm, careful not to interfere with his driving, feeling greatly reassured.

She was part of the family, and they were the only family she had left. Her true father, a Grand Prix racing driver, had been killed when Lexa was only three. She did not even remember him, although the tattered photo she had was very precious to her. Her mother had married Rex Fallon thirteen years later, but they had been married for only two years before Lexa's mother died.

Rex had always been kind, loving, accepting her as part of his family even though she had been away at school and college abroad for all the years she had known him. Now, her education, completed in Switzerland, was finished and she was going back to live with her stepfather.

For the past two years, since her mother died, in fact, she had not been back. Despite invitations from Rex, she had spent her Christmases and holidays at the houses of friends. Somehow she had been reluctant, afraid that perhaps she would not be accepted as part of Rex Fallon's family, now that her mother was dead. And if that had been the case, then she would have been completely on her own, a frightening thought and one that she had been unable to face.

But as it happened, Rex had telephoned her a couple of days before term ended. They had talked for an hour and he had asked her to come home. It *was* her home, he insisted, and this time Lexa had listened, accepted what he said, knowing that she did want to live with him and the family.

And so here she was, driving towards the lovely old house she remembered so well, longing to see everybody again.

It had been crazy to stay away so long. There had been no real reason, she knew that now, but when her mother had died she had felt so very alone, despite letters and telephone calls and visits from Rex, Nick and Marny. It had been a traumatic period of her life, one that she had only now finally pulled out of.

At last she could accept that they all cared for her, saw her as part of them even though there was no blood tie.

Did Jase care? she asked herself almost desperately. He had not phoned or written, she had not seen or heard from him for two years. She purposefully pulled her thoughts away from him.

'How's your music going?' she asked Nick, concentrating on him fiercely.

He played piano, was making quite a name for himself as a composer and, in his spare time, played in a successful jazz band.

'Great!' His face was bright with enthusiasm as he started to tell her all about it, but Lexa found her thoughts wandering.

It was strange how two brothers could be so unalike. Nick was younger, of course, only twenty-eight, while Jase was thirty-six, but even so, they were totally different.

Nick's personality was softer, uncomplicated. Jase was hard and forceful, very complex. She had always been closer to Nick, had always yearned to be closer to Jase.

But Jase had never been there. He had started building up his business empire as soon as he had left university. Now he was incredibly rich and successful and spent most of his time in America, and that was why it had been such a surprise to find that he was home. Her nerves tingled with anticipation as that thought flashed through her mind. Twenty years old and still acting like a teenage girl with a crush on some rock star! she told herself scathingly.

Then suddenly the car was turning off the narrow country road, cutting away her thoughts, as they drove through old wrought iron gates, down the long gravelled drive until the house came into view.

Lexa found that she was holding her breath, willing the place not have changed. It hadn't. It was exactly the same, an enormous, mellow stone house, with a white pillared porch, and climbing ivy, its long windows glinting in the bright afternoon sunlight.

She let out her breath. It was beautiful. Smiling at Nick, she jumped out of the car. The birds were singing, the sweet summer scent of the gardens filling her nostrils.

Then Nick was beside her. 'Welcome home, Lexa,' he said quietly, seriously, and kissed her, his lips cool and gentle against hers. She put her hands on his shoulders and kissed him back, very, very happy and totally unaware that a tall dark figure watched that kiss from a window above.

Nick took her hand and led her inside. 'I'll bring your cases in later—let's find Rex.'

They walked through the high quiet hall, still hand in hand. It smelled of flowers and polish, and Lexa gazed round at the pale walls, the large Chinese tapestries, the bowls of yellow roses.

'Does it feel like home?' Nick asked, his eyes on her small rapt face as she took everything in.

She nodded. 'Exactly like home.' From somewhere in the house she could hear saxaphone music, faint and low and soulful. 'Yes, it's more like home than I remembered.' She laughed, because that was what she always had remembered, the music, the life. Rex had filled the house with music and noise and freedom and people. Everybody did what they wanted, when they wanted. The atmosphere was happy and relaxed and worked on Lexa like magic, soothing her nerves and anxieties as they made their way towards Rex's study.

Her stepfather was at his desk working, his shaggy silver-grey head bent in concentration. As soon as the door opened he jumped to his feet, engulfing Lexa in his arms, holding her tightly.

'I'm so very glad you've come back, my child,' he said huskily as they smiled at each other.

'Me too. It's so good to see you, Rex.' Incredibly Lexa found that her eyes were filled with tears.

Rex looked older, thinner, yet surprisingly fit and healthy, the hard bones of his face, inherited by his sons, Jase and Nick, smooth and tanned. He certainly did not look ill.

'You'll want to rest, freshen up after your journey. Look after her, Nick.' He stroked Lexa's hair. 'We'll talk over coffee, later. Right?'

'Right,' she agreed happily, kissing his cheek, feeling a strong rush of affection for him.

'You know where your room is?' Nick teased, as they reached the bottom of the stairs.

'Is it . . . Is it still my room?' she asked breathlessly.

'Of course it is, you silly girl. I'll fetch your cases.'

He disappeared, and Lexa ran nimbly up the massive staircase. They had kept her room, and that meant a lot to her.

She pushed open the door and walked inside. The windows were open, the cane blinds pulled high, the sunshine pouring in. She looked around. Everything was how she had left it, even though she had never spent much time here. She looked at the pictures, the plants, the oak furniture, the bright patchwork quilt, with happiness.

There was a light knocking on her door and she jumped like a scared rabbit, immediately thinking of Jase. But it was Nick with her suitcases.

'Where shall I put them?'

'On the bed. Thanks for meeting me, Nick,' she said seriously.

'My pleasure.' His eyes skimmed over her warmly. 'I was only making sure you didn't chicken out at the last minute.'

'I might have done, but I'm glad I didn't now. I think I'll unpack and take a shower, I feel a wreck after that journey.'

'I'll see you later, then,' Nick said easily, moving to the door.

When he had gone, Lexa flipped open her suitcases, pulling out her clothes and hanging them in the wardrobes.

She suddenly caught sight of herself in one of the mirrors and stared at her reflection. A tall slim girl stared back at her, tousled blond curls falling to her shoulders, wide green eyes and a generous, vulnerable mouth. She looked different today.

Shaking her head, she finished unpacking her clothes and strolled out on to the balcony of her room. The gardens and the swimming pool lay below her. She lifted her face to the sun. Such a beautiful day, midsummer.

A movement in the trees at the edge of the gardens caught her eye. Three black Dobermans bounded from the shadows, across the grass towards the house, followed by a tall, powerfully built man. He was walking slowly, indolently, the sunlight gleaming on his black head. Jase. Lexa's heart seemed to stop beating for a second and she instinctively stepped back so that she could watch him without being seen herself, and followed every easy, graceful movement of his body as he approached the house, staring at his wide, powerful shoulders and broad chest, lean hips and strong legs, the proud set of his dark head.

A deep ache triggered in her stomach. She wanted to see him closer, wanted to look into his face. His name hovered on her lips, but she did not call him. She was suddenly shy, unsure of herself, unsure of his reaction if he saw her.

Instead, she strolled into her bathroom and turned on the shower taps. A cold shower, wasn't that what they always recommended?

Three-quarters of an hour later, she left her room, relaxed and refreshed, the fine cotton of her emerald

dress swirling around her slim legs as she ran
downstairs.

If Rex was not busy, she would take up his offer of
coffee and a chat. The hall was deserted. She made her
way towards the study, but as she approached she could
hear her stepfather talking on the telephone.

So she turned round, intending to come back later,
and cannoned into a hard male body. Strong hands
reached out to steady her and she looked up into the
shuttered golden depths of Jase's eyes.

'Hello, Lexa.' His voice was soft, strangely rough. He
did not seem at all surprised to see her.

'Hello, Jase.' It was barely whispered. She was
achingly aware of his nearness, his long hard fingers
curling around her bare arms. He was making no
move to release her and she could feel his eyes on
her, skimming over her loose golden hair, her golden
skin.

'I'm waiting to see Rex,' she said nervously, not quite
daring to meet his eyes, staring at the top button of his
shirt, at the curling dark hair on his tanned chest. Jase
did not answer. He was still staring at her.

'You're beautiful,' he said with a faint smile.

Startled by his husky words, she jerked her head up
and as their eyes met, she felt a physical shock, like an
electric current running through her body. She had been
waiting two years for this moment, and she gazed into
his face, almost unaware of her actions.

She remembered every detail with painful clarity. His
hair was long, brushed back from his face, thick and
black and vital. His face was strong-boned, tanned, his
mouth hard and sensual. But it was his eyes that held
her, narrowed, cynical, a strange gold colour. He was
compelling, devastatingly attractive, just to look at him
made Lexa's heart beat suffocatingly fast.

'Thank you.' She acknowledged his compliment with a gentle smile. 'I've had two years to grow up.'

'Are you back for good?' The question was casual, expressionless, yet she had the strange impression that he was waiting carefully for her answer.

'Yes ... I ...' She bit her lip, her green eyes shadowed and uncertain, fearful of rejection.

Jase's expression softened. 'I'm glad,' he said gently, his low voice shivering down her spine, raising the hair on the back of her neck. Her answering smile was brilliant with relief, and on impulse, she stretched up and kissed his tanned cheek.

She felt him stiffen almost imperceptibly, his hands dropping from her arms, and she cursed herself savagely, her small face running with embarrassed colour. Why on earth had she done that? Did his approval mean so much to her?

Jase sighed, his eyes on her downturned head. 'Lexa, for ...' he began roughly.

'There you are! I've been looking all over for you two.' Nick's voice broke between them like a jet of freezing cold water.

Lexa managed an embarrassed smile as he approached, feeling unbearably guilty as though she had been found doing something dreadfully wrong.

Nick's eyes moved from her to Jase and back again, sensing that he had interrupted something.

'What's happening?' he asked, too casually, too jovially.

Jase was silent, his stance vaguely threatening.

'I'm on my way to see Rex,' Lexa replied lightly, breaking the silence. There was tension in the air around them, binding the three of them in a dark, strange atmosphere. She stared at her two stepbrothers. Both were watching her. Jase's expression was blank, hooded, Nick's was suspicious, wary. She had the feeling that there was something going on, something she could not understand, and she heard the faint ring of the receiver being replaced from within the study, with a sigh of pure relief.

'Excuse me.' Without looking at either of them, she knocked on the door and entered to Rex's command.

'Are you busy?'

Her stepfather smiled at her, tidying papers on his desk. 'Just finished for today. Ready for that coffee we agreed on?'

Lexa nodded. 'Can we have it in the garden? It's such a lovely day. Shall I go and make it?' She was touchingly eager to please.

Ten minutes later they were sitting by the swimming pool, under the shade of a multi-coloured parasol, sipping fresh coffee. There was no sign of Jase or Nick, but Lexa could hear Nick playing the piano through one of the open windows. Something about his playing gave her the strong feeling that he was angry, and she felt puzzled. Surely he could not be angry because she had been talking to Jase? It didn't make sense.

She turned to Rex. 'What are you working on at the moment?'

He was a writer, famous for his historical biographies. They chatted about his work and Lexa poured more coffee for them both, but even as they talked and despite all her efforts, she found that her thoughts were on Jase. She was talking normally, even concentrating on what Rex was saying, yet part of her was filled with Jase.

He had told her she was beautiful. He was glad that she was back for good. That meant he cared, didn't it? Surely it did. A warm glow settled around her heart, lighting her eyes, giving brilliance to her smile.

'I really have come home,' she said, touching Rex's arm, as they finished their coffee.

'No regrets?' Rex took her hand in both of his, his pale eyes filled with affection.

'Not one,' Lexa said firmly. Then, taking a deep breath, she reached a sudden decision. She owed it to Rex to explain why she had not been back for two years. 'Can I explain something to you?' Rex nodded, smiling.

She chose her words carefully. 'I think it must have hurt you that I didn't come back, after ... after my mother's funeral ... She paused, thinking hard. Rex opened his mouth to speak, but she knew what he was about to say and cut in. 'Please, don't say anything—I feel I must explain to you how I felt at the time—I'd like you to understand.' Her eyes pleaded with him and he acquiesced, his expression telling her to continue. 'When you married, I was glad to come and live here, you were all so kind and welcoming, but I think the fact that I was away at school nine months of the year meant that we didn't get to know each other so well, it put distance between us. So, after the funeral—well, I felt very alone, and I also felt that I didn't know any of you well enough. I was afraid that perhaps I wouldn't be welcome, I'm not a blood relation, after all. I thought I must remind you of ...' Her voice trailed off uncomfortably. 'I haven't explained it very well, but do you understand what I mean?'

Rex nodded. 'There's something you must understand too. I think of you as my daughter. Of course you remind me of your mother, but you bring happy memories, not sad ones, and you're part of this family—you belong here. Now, have we got that straight?' His pale eyes twinkled at her.

'Yes.' Lexa felt as though a great weight had been

lifted from her shoulders and her last reservations were swept away. 'I knew that as soon as I got back here—I'd been wrong for two years—so silly.'

At that moment Marny arrived, running from the house towards them, her black hair flying behind her.

She was Rex's adopted daughter, three years older than Lexa, a good friend, almost a sister. Rex's family was large and complex. It was incredible that they all lived in such relaxed harmony.

'Lexa, you're back. Wonderful!' The two girls embraced each other fondly, then Marny kissed Rex's cheek. 'I've only just got back from Edinburgh. I did so want to be here when you arrived—you must tell me all your news. Any coffee left?' Marny was a whirlwind of brightness and colour, leaving people breathless and stunned and happy as she whirled through their lives.

Lexa stared at her. Marny was vivid and beautiful in a scarlet jump-suit and high-heeled sandals, her oval face perfectly made-up, her black hair shining in the sunlight. 'No coffee, I'm afraid. Shall I go and make some more?'

Nick whistled through his teeth from one of the sitting room windows. 'Rex—telephone!'

Rex stood up, sighing regretfully. 'No coffee for me, my child.'

'I'll see you later.' Lexa's eyes followed him as he walked back inside. She was immeasurably glad that they had talked. She turned to Marny. 'Coffee?'

The other girl nodded. 'Lovely!'

'Suits me fine too.' Nick was suddenly beside them, sliding into one of the low comfortable chairs, stretching his hands behind his head, his eyes on Lexa.

'So that's coffee for three.' She stood up and Marny piled cups on to the tray.

'Better make that four. I see my dear brother walking

this way,' Nick remarked lazily, as she picked up the tray.

Lexa turned her head involuntarily, watching Jase stroll along the side of the pool towards them. She was utterly captivated by the movements of his powerful body, so slow and graceful, so self-assured. He wore denim jeans, tight and faded, and a dark shirt open low at the neck. He exuded an air of wealth, of power and success, and she could not tear her eyes away from the magnificent primitive beauty of him.

His eyes met hers, blank, unfathomable, and she lowered her head, praying that her hands would not shake, disturbing the tray and giving her away.

She glanced at Marny and found that Marny was also watching Jase, a secret fascination in her black eyes.

Quickly turning away, Lexa walked towards the house, precariously balancing the tray, glad to be able to escape, bewildered by what she had seen in Marny's eyes.

She kept her head down as she passed Jase, not even looking at him, her face suddenly hot with colour that she did not want him to see.

Mrs Frone was in the huge kitchen, rolling out pastry on a floured board. She managed a half smile as Lexa entered, which was encouraging because Mrs Frone hardly ever smiled. 'Will it be okay for me to make some more coffee, Mrs Frone?' asked Lexa sweetly.

'Help yourself.' The housekeeper continued working.

Lexa ground some coffee beans, singing to herself, and while she waited for the percolator, she looked round the room.

Rex had had the whole house modernised when he bought it all those years ago, and the kitchen was a housekeeper's dream.

Mrs Frone, a widow in her late fifties, preferred 'the old ways', as she called them, but still appreciated the labour-saving devices that Rex had installed. She had been with the family for years. Nick had once jokingly told Lexa that he suspected Mrs Frone to be Rex's mother. She was ageless, the backbone of the wild carefree family, and they all loved her even while fearing her a little.

'Would you like a cup?' Lexa asked as she added extra cups to the tray.

'I don't mind if I do,' Mrs Frone replied in her flat endearing voice.

Smiling, Lexa poured out a cup, gave it to Mrs Frone with a sweet smile, and picking up the tray went back outside, the bright sun almost blinding her as she walked into it.

Jase was sitting with Marny and Nick now, his long legs stretched out in front of him, his eyes narrowed against the sun. Lexa noticed that Marny was still watching him. Both men were lazily smoking. Nick took the tray from her suddenly-trembling hands as she approached.

'You can pour, Marny,' he smiled, pushing the loaded tray towards her.

Lexa sat down next to Jase, the only available seat, her heart beating fast at his nearness, her mouth very dry.

'So how was Switzerland?' Marny asked excitedly, almost spilling the coffee, not watching it.

'Beautiful. I was sad to leave.'

'What are the men like? All tall silent mountaineering types?'

Jase and Nick both laughed, and glancing at Jase from the corner of her eye, Lexa could see him smiling at Marny with wry indulgence. She felt a faint stab of jealousy.

'I didn't get much chance to find out,' she replied, lighting a cigarette offered by Nick.

'I don't believe that for a second, you can tell me later—when we're alone.' Marny raised her eyebrows conspiratorially.

'Ah, secrets?' Nick laughed.

'You'll never know,' Marny smiled at him.

'Why do women discuss their love affairs so avidly with each other?' Nick complained half-jokingly.

'Women form stronger, more intimate friendships than men,' Marny replied with certainty, sticking out her tongue at him.

Jase raised his dark brows. 'Would you agree with that, Lexa?' His voice was cool, a low drawl, and she could feel him looking at her even though she did not turn her head.

'Yes, I think so. I don't know why it is, though.' She was thrown by his sudden attention, aware that she sounded stupid, inane. Knowing a flash of inexplicable panic, she got to her feet, feeling too affected by him to stay. She could not bear him to think her stupid, she could not bear to make a fool of herself. 'Excuse me, I think I'll go inside—I'm rather hot.' She walked away, aware that her abrupt behaviour had startled them all. She could feel their eyes on her back, but she did not care. She would think up an excuse later. It did not matter, she had to get away.

She had just reached the hall, intending to go up to her room, when hard fingers closed on her shoulders, turning her slowly to face Jase. Somehow, she was not surprised that he had followed her. She lowered her head, biting her lower lip.

'What's the matter?' he asked quietly.

'Nothing.' Her mouth was stubborn.

'You shot away like a scalded cat.' There was

laughter in his voice, belied by the relentless probe of his golden eyes.

'I'm hot and tired. I wanted to get out of the sun, that's all.'

His fingers were moving on her arm, stroking slowly over her soft bare skin, but she could tell that he was hardly aware of these actions.

'Okay.' Incredibly, he smiled at her.

Lexa stared at him, the warm, easy charm in his face making her catch her breath. 'Don't treat me like a child,' she said flatly, feeling inexplicably hurt. 'There's really no need to worry about me.'

'No?' He was clearly disbelieving, and she felt angry because he had no idea of the effortless hold he had on her emotions. He could make her so happy or he could destroy her, and he did not even know that.

'Just leave me alone,' she said, trying to keep her voice even. His fingers tightened on her arm, hurting her.

'Just give me one good reason why on earth I should,' he countered smoothly, though his eyes flashed anger at her.

'Why are you here?' she demanded curiously, ignoring his angry question.

'I came to see Rex, and perhaps I also came to see you.'

'You didn't know I'd be here,' she said in a small shocked voice, not really believing him.

'I knew you'd come back.' His voice was impassive.

'How?'

'You're very easy to read.' Hurt, she turned away. Did he know of her strange, confused yearning for him? She couldn't bear to think that he did.

'Am I?'

'Lexa, I'm not insulting you . . .'

'I suppose not,' she cut in flatly. Then, 'Am I really easy to read?'

'To me, yes, those beautiful, clear green eyes tell me everything.' Jase was smiling slightly, staring down at her.

She immediately lowered her head, but he slid his thumb under her chin and tilted up her face so that she could not avoid him.

'Have I changed since you last saw me?' she questioned breathlessly.

'Shall I tell you what you want to hear?' His mouth was hard and cynical.

'Don't be cruel,' she begged, gazing into the fierce golden depths of his eyes. She could read no expression in them, they were shuttered, totally blank.

'No, you don't deserve cruelty,' he murmured, tracing the line of her softly rounded jaw with his long fingers, almost surprised that she was so vulnerable. 'You're so beautiful, so sweet.'

Lexa stared at him, mesmerised, knowing for certain that while he murmured those deep compliments he was very angry inside, and she suddenly felt frightened.

'You're angry—why?' She was direct in her new fear. His fingers were still moving on her face, so very gently, burning like fire and ice against her skin.

'You're not a child any more. Surely you know?'

She shook her head, out of her depth now. Had she done something wrong?

'I want you, Lexa, that's why I'm angry—angry with myself for being a crazy, bloody fool.' Jase swore violently, his voice low, vibrant. His words echoed in her head like bells. Jase wanted her and yet that desire made him angry. She did not understand it.

The implications behind the savagely bitten out

words took longer to sink in, but when they did, she began to tremble violently.

Jase felt her trembling beneath his fingers and misread her reactions. 'I won't touch you,' he promised harshly, bitterly. 'You have nothing to worry about.'

They both heard Marny and Nick, their voices coming closer, their laughter threading the still, summer air.

Raging with conflicting emotions, Lexa tore herself away from Jase and ran like the wind upstairs.

CHAPTER TWO

THAT night at dinner, Lexa met Zack Harvey. He was a
friend of Nick's, a professional photographer, who
lived in London. Nick had invited him for the evening.

Zack was tall and blond, with laughing grey eyes, and
Lexa was under no illusions about him. He made it
obvious from the moment they met that he found her
very attractive.

Jase was abrupt, silent throughout the meal, despite
Marny's gentle teasing. Looking at him, Lexa found
that he was staring at her with dark brooding eyes. Her
stomach turned over as their glances locked, her eyes
widening, pupils dilating.

He broke the eye contact seconds later, turning away to
talk to Rex. She sipped her wine slowly, still watching
him. He looked fiercely attractive tonight in a
wine-coloured velvet jacket and black trousers. His hair
was neatly brushed, thick and dark against his tanned skin.

She could feel her blood stirring, quickening as she
looked at him and remembered the harsh words of
desire he had spoken that afternoon. He could not
possibly want her more than she wanted him, it was like
a terrible fever inside her.

Marny was also watching him, Lexa realised, the
other girl's dark eyes were mysterious, over-bright.
Marny wanted Jase too, she suddenly understood, with
a faint pang of shock. Such a mess, and she had been
back for less than twenty-four hours.

'You're looking awfully serious tonight,' Nick
murmured in her ear, diverting her.

Lexa smiled, her lips stiff. 'Sorry, I was deep in thought.'

'What were you thinking about?'

'Jase.' The truth had slipped out before she realised it, and Nick's mouth tightened.

'What's so fascinating about Jase?' There was a faintly sullen edge to his voice.

'Does he have lovers?' she asked guilelessly, her lightness veiling a deep curiosity.

'What do you think?' Nick snorted cynically. 'Women fall at his feet.'

'Are you jealous?' she smiled, gentle with understanding.

'I suppose I am.' His shoulders lifted self-deprecatingly, his good humour returning.

'Are you trying to tell me that women don't fall at your feet?' she teased.

'Chance would be a fine thing!'

'Is there anybody special, Nick?' she asked gently.

He nodded, surprising her.

'And she doesn't give a damn,' he admitted bitterly, a dull red flush creeping along his cheekbones.

'Oh, that's awful! I'm sorry.' Lexa's eyes were very tender as she looked at him and she wished that she had not probed, the wound had obviously not yet healed.

'Forget it. I'd rather not talk about it anyway.' His embarrassment was growing. 'But talking of romance, Zack is certainly smitten with you,' he added, changing the subject completely.

'He seems nice,' she replied rather noncommittally.

'Ah, he doesn't make your heart beat faster'

Lexa shook her head. Only Jase could do that. She had the deepest conviction that he was the only person who ever would, and it was very depressing.

In the background, breaking into her thoughts, she

could hear Marny teasing Jase, asking him why he was so grumpy. She turned back to Nick, determined not to listen, even though she knew Jase's eyes were resting on her.

After dinner, everybody retired to the drawing room for coffee and brandy. Nick played the piano, Rex was jovial, joking, and Marny sat with Jase, very close to him.

Lexa watched them covertly. Jase's mood seemed to have lightened. He looked relaxed now, his long hard body coiled indolently in a comfortable leather chair. He was smoking a cigar, the fragrant smoke drifting, spiralling from his beautifully-moulded lips. He was making Marny laugh.

Lexa talked with fierce concentration to Zack, guilty yet relieved when he rose to leave, explaining that he had a very early call the next morning.

She had parried and sidestepped all his invitations to go out and not wanting to hurt him, had finally given in and agreed to let him telephone her some time later in the week. He had seemed so grateful that she felt awful for using him as a shield against Jase.

When he had gone, she wandered out into the garden through the long french windows, with the dogs, sensing a walk, trailing at her heels.

It was a warm, balmy night, the flowers scenting the heavy air. Lexa walked through the darkness, the pale silk of her dress drifting around her body, listening to the piano music, the laughter from inside the house. She felt alone yet content. Her first day back had certainly been eventful, she reflected, as she walked towards the trees.

Now that her eyes were accustomed to the darkness, she realised that it was quite light, the moonlight giving the garden a ghostly monochrome sheen. She leant against a cool, rough tree trunk, staring up at the sky, her mind crowded, enjoying the light breeze against the skin of her face.

Lost in thought, she did not notice the silent approach of a shadowed figure until he was right in front of her.

'Jase.' She whispered his name, half frightened, half exhilarated. She had been thinking of him. Had her thoughts brought him to her? She almost believed that they had.

'You've been missed,' he said quietly. 'Rex sent me out to find you.'

'Oh.' So her thoughts hadn't brought him after all. He had not even come of his own free will, and she felt ridiculously piqued as she looked at him. His tie was gone, his shirt open at the neck. 'You can tell him I'm fine, just getting some night air. I'll be in later,' she said stiffly.

Jase ignored her, lighting a cigarette, the flare from the lighter illuminating the strong planes of his face for a second.

'Why are you out alone?'

'I've told you——'

'You told me how to placate Rex, now tell me the real reason,' he said coolly.

'I like to walk at night,' she muttered, feeling like a ticked off child.

'Alone?' he queried softly.

'Usually.' Her heart was pounding. Could he hear it? It sounded deafening. Afraid that he might be able to, she moved jerkily away, her foot tangled in an exposed root on the ground and with a stifled cry she felt herself falling.

Jase moved forward, lightning-fast, reaching for her, saving her.

Lexa let her hands rest on his wide shoulders as he set her on her feet again. She could feel the tensing of his powerful shoulder muscles beneath the fine velvet of his jacket. He released her abruptly, so abruptly that she almost fell again.

Regaining her balance, she glared at him. 'Thank you.' There was no mistaking the grudge in her voice. Jase smiled, his golden eyes warm and amused.

'You're too sensitive, Lexa. You'll have to toughen up if you want to survive,' he said gently, laughing.

'Advice seems to be one of your strong points, doesn't it?' she snapped, pulling a face at him, surprised when he laughed again, a low growl of genuine amusement.

'That was supposed to be insulting,' she said stiffly, suppressing the urge to laugh herself.

His dark brows rose. 'Really? You'll have to do better than that.' He was teasing her, coaxing her into a lighter mood, and she could not resist him, a small smile lifting the corners of her mouth.

'I suppose I will. Your skin seems to be as thick as a rhinoceros's, Jase Fallon!'

He smiled at her and they began walking through the trees together. The silence that grew between them was, for once, not tense or strained, but harmonious, almost companionable. Jase watched her from beneath hooded eyelids as she walked so gracefully beside him. The pale silk of her dress wrapped by the breeze around her slender body, gave her a pure ethereal beauty, and he felt his blood stirring deeply inside him. His fists clenched by his sides as he fought for, and attained, control.

'What will you do with your life, Lexa?' he asked evenly, quietly.

'I don't know. I suppose I have no ambition.' A

thought struck her like an arrow. 'But I have no
intention of sponging off Rex for the rest of my life, if
that's what you're getting at.'

'That's not what I was getting at at all. Heavens, you
are a bad-tempered child! Why do I need to choose
every word so carefully with you?' His voice was rough
again and it seemed that their period of easy
companionship was over.

Lexa wished she had not jumped to such an unjust
conclusion. Of course Jase had not been hinting that
she was using Rex as an easy meal-ticket, and she
wished she was not so edgy and defensive with him.

'I'm sorry, Jase,' she said very quietly, her eyes pure
and sincere, finding his.

'Forget it.' His momentary anger was gone; perhaps
she did have some power over him after all, over his
moods, his reactions. For some reason, she wanted to
think so, and more than that, she wanted to make
things right between them again, by explaining her
position.

'I really don't know what I'll do; I've been thinking
about it for months now. I certainly don't want to go
on to university. What I think I'll do is try to get a job,
any job, while I decide what I really want to do, then
work towards my chosen career.'

Jase lit another cigarette with swift easy movements.

'You could work for me,' he suggested expressionlessly, after a small pause.

'In America?' Her voice mirrored her surprise.

'In New York or here in London—the choice would
be yours.'

'Doing what?'

'Office work to start off with, I'm afraid, but only
while you learned the business. It would give you time
to think, to decide what you wanted.'

Lexa stared at him, wide-eyed, suddenly a little scared of the future.

'Thank you. I'll think about it and let you know,' she promised breathlessly, happy at his kindness. If she had the choice, as he said she did, then she would choose New York because it would be nearer to him, and yet if she did choose New York it would mean leaving Rex again. She shook her head. She would think about it later, when she was alone. Right now she wanted to take full advantage of being in Jase's company without the problems of decision-making.

'Do that, and let me know before I fly back,' he replied, deftly pushing aside some bushes so that she would not rip her dress. That stopped Lexa dead in her tracks.

'When . . . when will you be flying back?' she asked miserably.

His wide shoulders lifted. 'In a couple of weeks, maybe longer.' Lexa was silent. She didn't want him to go back, she wanted him to stay.

'And what about marriage and children, do they figure in your future plans, Lexa?' he asked suddenly.

'Oh yes, I want to find true love,' she replied softly. 'I want to spend my life with somebody I love, and have children.'

Jase smiled at the dreams in her eyes. 'Anybody in particular?' He was staring at her intently.

She flushed. He was the man who filled her dreams, but she could not tell him that.

'No . . . no, not yet,' she stammered.

His eyes narrowed perceptively. 'Now why do I get the feeling you're not telling me the truth?' he drawled softly.

'I am,' she protested, crossing her fingers behind her back. Did she love Jase? Everything seemed to add up that way. 'And what about you?' She tried to divert the conversation from herself. 'Will you marry? Will you have children?'

He did not answer immediately, and Lexa stared at his hard, unyielding profile, her heart turning over. Was he already in love with somebody? Nick reckoned he had women by the score, they fell at his feet. Just as I would, given the chance, she thought, with a flash of realisation.

The eyes he finally turned on her were dark and enigmatic. 'Who knows?' he drawled softly.

'How obtuse you are!' she complained with a sweet smile. 'Are you in love?'

'So direct!' he teased gently. 'Don't you know, my love, that you don't ask that sort of question?'

'Obviously not.' Her voice was sulky. It seemed certain that he had no intention of telling her whether or not he was in love, and it was burningly important that she knew.

'Jase, why didn't you write to me while I was in Switzerland?' Why was she asking that? She was only leaving herself open to be hurt, and Jase could hurt her so easily, a careless word, a cold glance, that was all it took.

'I was busy,' he answered flatly. 'And besides, I don't write letters.' She had well and truly asked for that, she thought, swallowing back the sudden rush of hot tears that rose in her throat.

Jase caught her shoulders suddenly, his fingers hard, biting into her soft flesh.

'Look at me,' he ordered, when she hung her head.

His voice brooked no argument, compelling her to obey, and she lifted her head slowly, staring into the strong lean lines of his face. His mouth was tight, a hard line, his eyes blank, as always.

'Don't try to turn me into some kind of saint, Lexa—you're asking for trouble if you do,' he warned in a low harsh voice.

'I haven't. . . .'

'Oh yes, you have. Those beautiful green eyes give you away every single time.'

She sank her teeth into the softness of her lower lip, feeling terribly hurt. Why was he being so cruel?

'You . . . you said you wanted me this afternoon,' she said brokenly, meeting his stormy eyes again.

'Yes, and I'm not denying that I want you, you're very desirable, but there are other women I want just as much. Don't read too much into what I say,' he told her, in that rough violent voice.

The painful blow of his words registered in her wide eyes, darkening them as they filled with tears.

'Lexa,' he groaned her name. 'For Pete's sake, don't cry!'

'You're hurting me,' she muttered, unable to stop the tears now, though she badly wanted to. They were suddenly flooding down her face. Jase abruptly released his steel-strong grip on her shoulders and in an easy convulsive movement, pulled her against his chest, bending her golden head to the hard width of his shoulder, his fingers gently threading through her soft curls as he let her cry.

All the events of the day, the long journey, the strain of facing Rex and the rest of the family after such a long time, Jase's hard words, all crowded in on her, breaking the floodgates of pent-up emotion, and she sobbed her heart out against his shoulder.

Jase gently stroked her hair, murmuring deep words of comfort, holding her tightly until her tears dried up. Lexa clung to him until there was no further reason for her to be in his arms.

Reluctantly she raised her head. Jase's shadowed eyes were tender as he wiped the last tears from her face before releasing her.

'We'd better get back to the house,' she said quietly, embarrassed that she had cried so openly, cringing when she remembered what she had said to him, what he had said to her, wishing that she had not shown him how easily hurt she was.

Jase nodded, taking her hand. She wanted to pull her hand out of his, but to do so would be to admit something that she did not want him to know. It was very impersonal, she told herself sternly, and let herself enjoy the warm touch of his fingers around hers.

The walked back to the house in silence. Glancing at Jase's profile, Lexa could not even guess at his thoughts. He seemed serious, preoccupied. She still felt hurt, sad, yet part of her knew that she had made a fool of herself, had laid herself open for his condemnation.

As they reached the swimming pool, Jase turned to her.

'I didn't mean to be so cruel, it was never my intention to hurt you,' he said softly, huskily. 'I'm sorry, Lexa.'

'It doesn't matter, you didn't hurt me.' Her voice was too bright, too light, and it fell between them on the soft night air, with them both knowing the truth.

Jase sighed. 'I'm glad to hear it,' he murmured sardonically, staring at her intently, unable to take his eyes off her.

She reached up and touched his cheek, her eyes shining, very beautiful, and as though he could not help himself, Jase caught her hand, pressing his mouth to the small palm. She shivered, the touch of his lips against her skin tingling along all her nerve endings.

His dark head seemed to lower in slow motion, his cool clean breath fanning her cheek, and her eyes closed as his mouth touched hers for the first time, brushing her lips gently, unhurriedly. But as her lips parted, he immediately raised his head, breaking the kiss.

Still in the grip of the incredibly sweet sensations induced by the brief touch of his mouth, Lexa stood perfectly still for a second before turning on her heel and running into the house without a word, without a backward glance.

The huge drawing room was deserted and she ran through the hall and up the stairs to her room, not even stopping to draw breath until the door was shut behind her.

Following her instincts, she walked over to the windows and out on to the balcony, looking down.

Jase was exactly where she had left him, standing by the swimming pool. He was idly smoking, staring down at the still water. Knowing that she could not be seen, Lexa watched him, a sharp tearing pain around the region of her heart as she stared down at his proud dark head.

He stood alone for about ten minutes, then grinding out his cigarette beneath the heel of his shoe, turned and walked out of view, into the house.

Lexa walked back into her bright bedroom thinking about the night's events. Jase had made it perfectly clear that he had no intention of becoming involved with her. She could not blame him for that even though it hurt her. He desired her, but as far as he was concerned, that was all. He had also made that humiliatingly clear.

She had been flinging herself at him ever since she had first seen him that afternoon. She could not help her feelings, but she decided that in future she would make every effort to hide them. There was no way she was going to give Jase the chance to hurt her again.

She wandered into her bathroom, trying to decide whether or not to take a bath. She knew for certain that she would not sleep if she went to bed now.

She touched her fingers to her lips, staring at her reflection in one of the mirrors. His kiss had been earth-shattering. She had never been kissed like that before. She had never experienced such deep aching feelings before, either. When other men had kissed her, it had been pleasant enough, but nothing, *nothing*, compared to the touch of Jase's mouth.

'I don't want to fall in love with him,' she told herself out loud, but she had the feeling that it was too late, there was something inevitable about the confused feelings she had for him.

He would hurt her, not deliberately, of course, but she could never be part of his life. He was her stepbrother, he probably thought she had some sort of adolescent crush on him.

Sighing, she began to remove her make-up, turning on the bath taps before she started. As she relaxed in the warm scented water, her mind drifted back to the first time she had met Jase.

She had been sixteen years old, a child. She had only heard stories of him from her mother, from Rex and Nick. He had been working in New York but had flown over for the wedding, and he had taken her breath away when she finally met him.

He had been courteous, polite, very kind to her. She had watched him all through the wedding service, all through the reception party afterwards. He was the sort of romantic hero one read about in books, but never ever met.

She realised now, looking back, that he had treated

her with gentle indulgence. She had been a child then, but now she was a woman, and she wanted more than his indulgence, much more. During the past four years she had not seen much of him—brief holidays, Christmas, that sort of thing, but he had never been far from her thoughts, never.

Still sighing loudly, Lexa climbed out of the bath and dried herself, pulling on a satin nightgown with careless hands. Her feelings were confused and her head would just not clear.

A light tapping on her bedroom door broke into her reverie. 'Come in!' Her whole body tensed as the door opened. But it was Marny, and she let her breath out in a gasp of relief.

'Am I disturbing you?'

'No, I can't sleep anyway. Come in.' Marny wandered into the room, shuddering at the moths that had flown in through the open windows and were winging blindly around the lamps.

'Where did you get to after dinner?' Marny asked, sitting down on the bed and pushing back her black hair.

Lexa shrugged. 'I went for a walk, I felt like some air.'

'Zack Harvey seems keen,' Marny remarked.

'Mmm.' Lexa tugged a brush through her tousled curls.

'Not interested?' Marny eyed her curiously.

'Not really. He seems nice enough, though.'

'He doesn't seem the type to give up easily, you'll probably have a fight on your hands.'

Lexa grimaced expressively. 'I hope not, I'm no good at that sort of thing!'

Marny laughed. 'I should be asleep by now, I have to be up at six,' she admitted ruefully.

'How's the job going?' Lexa asked with genuine interest.

'It's hard work. Everybody warned me that modelling wasn't as glamorous as it seemed—I had no idea how unglamorous it really is.'

'But you do enjoy it?'

Marny wrinkled her nose. 'On and off. I don't enjoy the dog-eat-dog competition and it's a very precarious business, but yes, I love it.'

'You are lucky,' Lexa said wistfully. 'I don't know what I want to do. Jase offered me a job tonight.'

'Tell!' Marny's eyes were suddenly avid, excited.

'An office job, that's all. I suppose I ought to take it, jobs aren't exactly easy to come by these days, but I don't feel very enthusiastic about it, I must admit,' Lexa confided.

Marny's eyes became slumbrous. 'I'd jump at the chance of working with Jase. I might ask him myself.' She saw Lexa's shocked expression and laughed. 'Come on, you've got to admit that he's something special. I think I'm in love with him!'

Lexa was silent. Aren't we all? she felt like saying, and hysterical laughter bubbled into her throat at the sheer ridiculousness of the whole situation.

'Honestly?' she managed at last.

Marny's eyes were dark, almost desperate. 'I'd do anything to get close to Jase, he's been in my blood for years. He's so damned cool, though. . . .' She seemed to make an effort to pull herself together. 'Sorry, Lexa, you must think I'm insane.'

'No. . . .'

'I only came in to say welcome home. It's lovely having you back and I didn't get the chance to tell you before.' Marny jumped off the bed, a faint flush along her high, perfect cheekbones, as though embarrassed that she had said too much. 'Shall we go up to London for lunch one day this week? I bet you're dying to do some shopping.' The old, bright Marny was back, a little tense, a little brittle, but well under control.

'Yes, that would be lovely. Whenever you're free,' Lexa smiled.

'Great! We'll make arrangements tomorrow. I must get to bed now, otherwise I'll be dead in the morning. Goodnight.'

'Goodnight, Marny.'

As soon as she had gone, Lexa sunk down on to the bed, stunned by what Marny had told her. Was the older girl really in love with Jase? She remembered the way Marny watched him whenever they were together. Poor Marny! Feel sorry for yourself, a tiny voice inside her head told her. Marny was strong, very beautiful, she always got what she wanted, and if she wanted Jase. . . .

Lexa flung herself between the cool smooth sheets, resting her hands behind her head. Jase was stronger than Marny, he would never be pushed. Never.

She switched off the lights and closed her eyes tightly, not in the least sleepy now. Had Jase kissed Marny the way he had kissed her tonight? Had he warned Marny not to turn him into a saint? She laughed out loud. Jase probably spent his whole life beating off young women who thought themselves in love with him. It served him right for being so damned attractive.

She wondered where he was at that moment. Was he working, was he asleep? At least he was in the same house, under the same roof as her. It was a step nearer.

She suddenly remembered something—she had not said goodnight to Rex. She sat up in bed. She had seen the study light from the garden, so her stepfather must still be working. She should not have forgotten. So she jumped out of bed, glad to have something to do. She would collect some books to read while she was downstairs, she decided, pulling on a thin satin peignoir. She needed something to while away the time if she couldn't sleep.

As she approached the study, creeping through the silent house, she could hear the sound of a typewriter from within. Rex was still working. Lexa tapped lightly on the door and stuck her head in. 'Can I come in?'

Her stepfather looked up from his work, a ready smile on his face.

'I thought you were in bed.'

'I realised I hadn't said goodnight to you.' She moved into the room. 'Working late?'

'Yes, I want to get this chapter finished tonight.'

Lexa ran her finger along the carved edge of the old desk. 'You shouldn't work so hard.'

'Has Nick been talking to you?' Rex demanded shrewdly.

'Well. . . .' She couldn't help smiling.

'It's a lot of nonsense and you mustn't take a blind bit of notice of him. Slowing down indeed!'

'He worries about you.'

Rex grunted, tapping his silver head expressively. 'I intend to keep my mind active, even if this old body is grinding to a halt.'

'You're impossible!' Lexa dropped a kiss on his cheek. He would not take advice, not from her or Nick or even Mrs Frone. She might as well give up. She sat down. Rex glanced at her, sensing that she needed to talk.

'Enjoyed your first day back?'

She nodded, smiling. 'It's as though I've never been away.' There was a slight pause, then she said, 'Jase offered me a job tonight.'

'Will you take it, do you think?'

'I don't know. He said I could work in New York if I wanted to.'

'And you're worried about leaving us again so soon?' He cut straight to the heart of her problem.

'Yes, that's the main thing, but I don't know whether or not I want the job—I don't know whether or not I want to work for Jase.' Betraying colour washed up over her small face as she spoke his name.

'You've argued?'

'No ... no, not exactly, well ... I. ...' She faltered into silence, unable to tell Rex what had really happened.

'Jase would be a good employer. He's strong, fair-minded, he wouldn't let you down, and he'd look after you,' Rex said slowly, misunderstanding the situation.

'Yes.' Lexa sighed. She knew all that. How could she expect Rex to help if she did not tell him everything?

'I'm going to think about it, anyway,' she said firmly, smiling.

'I can't help you make the decision, you're on your own, I'm afraid, my child. But you have all the time in the world, there's no rush. I didn't expect you to get a job as soon as you arrived here. Take your time, and remember that Jase is very fond of you.'

'It's good to have someone to talk it over with—thanks.' She suddenly felt very tired, exhaustion creeping up on her and hitting her like a bomb. She struggled to her feet, suppressing a yawn. 'Goodnight, Rex.'

He kissed her. 'Sleep well.'

'Don't work too hard,' Lexa said impishly, as she crept out into the darkness of the hallway.

She was tiredly climbing the stairs when Jase silently appeared at her side. His eyes narrowed, sliding slowly over the revealing satin of her nightclothes.

'You look dead on your feet,' he remarked drily.

'Thanks, Jase.' She managed a slight exhausted smile, her eyes drawn to the darkness of his face, and because she was not looking where she was going, her foot caught in the hem of her nightdress and she stumbled, almost falling down the stairs. Jase caught her—the second time that night, she realised, feeling stupid, and a moment later, she found herself being swung into his arms, her head suddenly against his chest.

'What ... what are you doing?' she demanded breathlessly.

'I get the distinct impression that you're not going to make it on your own,' he murmured in amusement against her golden hair.

She could not think of a thing to say, so she relaxed against the hard strength of his body, feeling the power in the tense muscles of the arms around her, knowing a fierce stab of pleasure at being so near to him, as he carried her effortlessly to her room, kicking open the door and laying her gently on the bed. She was just about to speak when he bent over her and touched his mouth gently to her forehead.

'Goodnight, Lexa.'

Then he was gone, leaving her wide-eyed, speechless and rather happy.

CHAPTER THREE

Two days later, Lexa woke early. It was barely dawn, the sky tinged with a deep golden pink, the birds singing loudly, sweetly. She glanced at the clock at her bedside and grimaced. It was far too early to get up, yet she knew that she would not sleep again.

She lay on her back staring at the ceiling, thinking of Jase, as usual. She had not seen him since he had carried her to her bed on that first day—he had gone to Birmingham on business, Rex had informed her the day before. The place was empty without him, and she longed for him to come back.

Sighing, she shifted restlessly between the silken sheets, then on a sudden impulse jumped out of bed and pulled a black bikini out of the wardrobe. She slipped it on, pushing her arms into a towelling robe, and quietly opening her bedroom door, went downstairs and outside.

It was a beautiful morning. The dogs, who had been lying at the bottom of the stairs, followed her out into the garden, tails wagging, eagerly expecting a walk.

Lexa dived cleanly into the still swimming pool, the exhilarating coldness of the water making her gasp, and swam the length of the pool twice, gradually becoming accustomed to the water, watching the clouds.

The splash behind her did not register until a tanned hand curled round her ankle, pulling her down into the water.

She surfaced seconds later, spluttering, to find Jase in

front of her, his powerful brown shoulders spilling water like diamonds, his black head gleaming.

'Oh, you . . . you . . .!'

'Don't say it, Lexa,' he warned laughingly, reaching out and pushing her wet hair from her face with gentle fingers. 'When did you get back?' Suddenly the day was brighter, she felt full of life. 'Very early this morning. And what are you doing up at dawn?' His voice was teasing.

She was staring at the cloud of dark hair curling from his brown chest, at the powerful muscles of his forearms. She had never seen him without a shirt before, and the sight of his naked, muscular body left her dry-mouthed, breathless and strangely weak.

'I . . . I couldn't sleep,' she stammered, lifting her gaze and smiling at him.

Those hooded golden eyes met hers, they were cool, searching, unreadable. They stared at each other for a few seconds, the atmosphere suddenly explosive, then Lexa turned away and swam down the pool, levering herself up the steps and out of the water.

She still felt a little worried about what Jase had said to her two nights before. She had been apprehensive about seeing him again, wondering how it would be between them. But it seemed as though it was going to be all right, she thought with happy relief.

She turned her head and watched Jase, his brown body cutting swiftly and powerfully through the water as rapidly he swam four lengths of the pool, her attention riveted on the pure animal grace of his movements.

She reached for a towel and rubbed her hair, her arms above her head, jumping as the towel was suddenly pulled from her unresisting fingers.

Jase gently dried her back, her shoulders, and she

stood stiffly, unresistingly, her heart pounding. Then he turned her to face him. His face was very serious, his eyes shadowed with emotion.

'Jase. . . .' She whispered his name, unable to hide her thoughts, her feelings, they shone in the green depths of her eyes as she stared up at him.

Easily reading her face, her eyes, he looked at her, his breath rasped harshly on the quiet morning air and seconds later he pulled her against his body, in one swift easy movement, his hands curving around her narrow waist.

His mouth found hers hungrily, parting her lips with deep expertise, and he was kissing her fiercely, almost desperately.

Lexa's response was mindless, her lips moving innocently beneath his warm mouth, her body yielding against the tense hardness of his. She slid her hands up to his shoulders, stroking the firm damp skin, a weak languid fever spreading like fire through her body leaving her clinging to him.

His mouth left hers, trailing tiny hungry kisses along the smooth line of her jaw, down the ivory column of her throat. He was breathing deeply, she could feel his quickening heartbeat striking up against her breasts.

His mouth was at her earlobe now, teasing it with his tongue, his white teeth, making her shiver convulsively.

'You're driving me insane,' he murmured huskily against her skin. 'I knew that as soon as I touched you, I wouldn't be able to leave you alone. Lexa——' His mouth found hers again, warm, seeking, coaxing an achingly passionate response from her. Lexa could feel his hands moving, stroking the bare skin of her waist, the curve of hips, his fingers burning her skin where they touched it. Her hands were following their own journey of exploration across Jase's tense, smooth-skinned back. His skin was cool, wet from the pool. She could feel his strength, the power of his body, desire uncontrolled inside her.

'Well, well, well, what's going on here?' Nick's cold mocking voice washed over them, immediately stiffening Lexa in Jase's arms. Jase lifted his dark head slowly, his arms tightening around Lexa's body, making no move to release her. He stared at his brother.

'What the hell do you want, Nick?' he demanded roughly.

Lexa leant her hot cheek against his shoulder, feeling more embarrassed than she had ever done before in her life. She looked at Nick and the desire raging inside her was doused as quickly as a match being plunged into cold water. He was staring at them both as though he couldn't believe his eyes. His mouth was tight, his expression condemning.

'You haven't wasted much time, have you, brother? She's only been home two days,' he remarked bitterly, a certain challenge in his brown eyes.

'Leave it, Nick,' Jase advised harshly.

'You bastard——'

'I said, leave it.' Jase's voice was deadly. Lexa could feel the tension in him, the threat of violence. Nick saw it too, taking a step backwards, his face flushing, his expression still sullen, bitterly angry. He would not back down, Lexa saw, it was a matter of pride. She couldn't stand it. Why were they fighting like this? She had the feeling that it went much deeper than this one sordid episode, and if that was the case, she wanted no part of it, she would not be used in their private quarrel.

'Stop it, both of you!' she shouted, tearing herself out of Jase's arms, her face pale and stricken as she looked from one to the other.

'Come off it, Lexa ...' Nick began with insulting mockery.

She saw Jase move like lightning, swinging back his tanned arm, his fist connecting with Nick's jaw, producing a sickening crack.

'No! Jase, don't. ...' She tried to get between them, sure that Jase could kill his brother without even trying, his strength was so vastly superior.

Nick was sprawled on the grass, rubbing his jaw. The side of his mouth was bleeding, but one look at him told Lexa that he was not beaten. Even as she watched, he was getting to his feet ready to fight.

'Jase, please!' She tried to grab his arm, but he easily shook her off.

'Stay out of this, Lexa,' he warned softly. He did not even look at her. He was staring at Nick, cool, totally in control, his body poised, tensed for promised violence. She might as well have not been there, and she felt very frightened as she watched them both.

She had to stop them, but she could not do it on her own. They would not listen, and she certainly did not have the physical capabilities to break them up. She had to get help. Turning on her heel, she ran back towards the house, praying that Rex would be up. There was no one else.

In answer to her prayers, incredibly, Rex was actually coming down the stairs as Lexa rushed into the hall. She was breathless, more with fear than physical exertion, and she collapsed against the banister.

'What is it, Lexa? Are you ill?' His face was creased with concern as he quickened his pace to reach her.

'It's Jase—and Nick—they're fighting—by the swimming pool!' she got out in short gasps.

'*What?*' It was clear that he was having difficulty believing it, but one look at her stricken face sent him striding through the drawing room towards the pool, with Lexa close behind him.

It was all over by the time they got there. Nick pushed past Lexa and Rex, as they reached the windows, holding a handkerchief to his mouth. He did not even glance at them. Jase was standing by the pool, lighting a cigarette. He seemed unhurt, still very calm, almost unmoved by the violent incident.

'What the hell's going on here?' Rex demanded, his voice furious.

Jase turned slowly, his golden eyes flicking blankly over them both, coming to rest on Lexa.

'I thought I told you to stay out of it,' he remarked coldly, his gaze burning through her.

'I couldn't,' she whispered, close to tears now. 'I was afraid.' She could not bear his censure.

'Jase, I want an explanation.' Rex was losing his temper. 'You've frightened this poor child half to death!'

Shaking her head blindly, Lexa turned on her heel and walked quickly away. Damn the lot of them! If they wanted to tear themselves to pieces that was their business; she did not want to be involved, it hurt too much.

Marny was in the drawing room, hovering, her black hair tousled, wearing only a thin silk nightdress.

'What on earth's going on?' she demanded, as Lexa came in. 'What's the matter with Nick? His mouth is bleeding and he's in one hell of a temper, and what's all the shouting?' Her dark eyes fixed curiously on Lexa. 'Lexa, are you all right? You're crying!'

Putting her hand up to her face, Lexa realised that it was wet with tears. She had not even noticed.

'I . . . I can't talk now. . . .' she sobbed, and walked past Marny, up the stairs to her room.

She met Nick on the landing, staring at him almost fearfully as they came face to face. He did not speak, merely looked at her and walked past.

She went into her room, and flinging herself on the bed, cried her heart out. It was so unfair!

She had no idea what was really happening, yet she was caught up in the middle of it all.

Jase had kissed her, that was all, a simple, beautiful kiss, and it had led to these dreadful scenes, this awful atmosphere, the shocking violence between two brothers. It was crazy, absolutely crazy, and she was hurt and very confused. But worse than all that was the fact that Jase was angry with her, and she did not know why. That was what hurt most.

She cried until all her tears were gone, then lay on the bed glaring at the wall. She heard the tapping on her door but ignored it, only moving when Marny's hand gently touched her shoulder.

'I've brought you some coffee. Are you all right, Lexa? Is there anything I can do?' She sounded so worried that Lexa rolled over on to her back and sat up.

'Yes,' she answered dully, 'I'm all right.'

Marny handed her the coffee in silence, her beautiful face twisted with concern.

Lexa sipped it gratefully. 'Thanks.' She blew her nose and wiped her eyes. They felt red and swollen and very uncomfortable.

'Rex and Jase are still shouting at each other,' Marny told her with a sigh. 'I can't stand scenes like this.'

'Me neither.' Lexa carried on sipping her coffee. It was calming her down, making her feel more human. I wish I hadn't got out of bed this morning,' she muttered, half to herself.

'What's going on?' Marny asked again, her voice pleading, lost.

Lexa shrugged. 'Don't ask me. Jase and Nick were fighting, so I got Rex—I didn't know what else to do—and Jase is angry with me now.' She was amazed at how calm she sounded.

'*Fighting?*' Marny's eyes were round, very shocked.

'It was awful, absolutely awful!' Lexa shuddered, not wanting to remember.

'But why?'

'I don't know,' Lexa said truthfully. Even from her bedroom they could hear the shouting downstairs. Rex sounded livid, out of control, Jase sounded hard and very cold.

Marny shook her head. 'I think the best thing we can do is to stay out of the way until this is all over. Can I stay here with you?'

Lexa nodded. She wanted to clap her hands over her ears to drown out the noise of the argument going on below. She could not hear what they were saying, but the noise was horrific enough. Marny was upset, Lexa could tell just by looking at her.

'I wish I had a radio,' she said, smiling weakly at the older girl.

'I've got one in my room. Shall I get it?'

'If you dare,' Lexa grimaced.

Marny walked to the door, sticking her head out and looking both ways along the landing before stepping outside. She returned within minutes carrying a small portable radio. She put it on Lexa's dressing table and switched it on. The bright, empty music drowned out all the noise from downstairs and they smiled at each other, both of them still a little frightened, a little hysterical.

They listened halfheartedly to the music, chatting in a strained kind of way for about a quarter of an hour. Lexa wanted to laugh, the whole situation was so utterly ridiculous. Jase and Rex were involved in a bitter argument downstairs, while she and Marny listened to the radio, consciously not becoming involved, trying to pretend that nothing was happening.

Finally, Marny switched off the radio and they both strained their ears to listen. The silence was deafening.

'Seems like it's all over,' Marny said with relief.

'I hope so,' Lexa said fervently. 'Oh no! Look at the time—I'll have to dash, see you later.' She rushed towards the door, and when she had gone, Lexa took a shower, moving slowly, automatically, deep in thought.

Now that her fear and horror were wearing off, she was beginning to feel the first faint stirrings of anger at what had happened. How dared Jase and Nick use her like this? Jase was so cold and so angry, she did not need him to fight her battles, she could have handled Nick herself. There had been no need for that punch. Nick had been rude, he'd been insulting, but she felt now that in part, she had perhaps deserved it. It must have been a shock for him to come upon her entwined in Jase's arms, responding so passionately to him. Yes, she felt sure that she could have handled it.

She dressed carelessly in blue jeans and a white peasant style blouse, then pulled a brush through her hair, grimacing at her reflection in the mirror. Her eyes still looked a little swollen, her face pale, drawn. Too bad. She didn't particularly care.

The dining room was empty, which was a great relief. She couldn't face any food, so she poured herself some coffee and lit a cigarette, which seemed to help her ravaged nerves.

She felt tense, jumpy, expecting one of the family to appear at any second, and she felt totally unable to face any of them. What would Rex say? Would he blame her? She drank a second cup of coffee swiftly, and anxious to get out of the house for a while, decided to go for a long walk. The grounds of the house were extensive, she could easily lose herself for a couple of hours without anybody finding her.

Wandering out of the long french windows, she picked up speed as she passed the pool, walking across the lawns towards the trees.

It was warm and bright, she could smell the grass and the flowers, she could hear insects buzzing loudly on the quiet air.

She walked until she reached the river. It was quite a way from the house, on the very edge of the grounds, one of her favourite places. She always came here when she wanted to be alone, when she was upset or miserable. It was her refuge.

She gazed at the clear, fast-running water, at the smooth brown stones on the river bed. Overhead, a plane left a trail of white in the bright blue sky, the low roar drifting on the edge of her thoughts.

She sat down, leaning back against a tree trunk, the sharp grass tickling her bare ankles, and closed her eyes. The sun was having a soporific effect on her, the warmth, the stillness, the peace, the gentle gurgling of the river, all combining to make her drowsy, her eyelids drooping lazily. She was not going to fall asleep, she told herself vaguely, she was just relaxing. . . .

She was dreaming. Jase was with her and she felt very, very happy. He was touching his mouth to her forehead, stroking her hair very gently. She sank into a light golden mood, content to know that he was with her.

She opened her eyes slowly, blinking in the relentless sunlight, stretching her arms above her head, her body arching like a satisfied cat, and focusing her eyes, found herself gazing into the lean, guarded lines of Jase's face. Her arms dropped, her body stiffening. He was standing a few feet away from her, his hands thrust casually into the pockets of his tight jeans, and he was staring at her.

Lexa cursed the colour that she could feel coursing up her face. Jase smiled, a slight softening of his beautifully-moulded mouth, and she dragged her eyes away from his, lowering her head.

Had she imagined that warm gentle kiss, had she been dreaming or had it been reality? She would probably never know, because she was far too embarrassed to ask.

She lifted her hand, pushing it through her soft curls, shading her eyes as she dared to look at him again.

'What are you doing here?' Her voice only shook a little.

'Looking for you,' came the faintly amused reply.

'How did you know . . .?'

'This is where you always used to come. I guessed you'd be here.' He was still staring at her, unnerving her.

'How clever of you,' she said flatly, turning away from him again, wishing that he would go away, surprised that he had remembered. It made her angry that her heart was beating faster, that the mere sight of him could take her breath away.

'No, not so damned clever,' he said with soft irony, raking a hand through the darkness of his hair.

Lexa's eyes jerked to his strong face. 'What does that mean?'

'It means that I want to apologise for upsetting you this morning. That scene with Nick——' He sighed heavily. 'It shouldn't have involved you. I'm sorry you got mixed up in it.'

'Not half as sorry as I am,' she replied sadly. 'Is it all over now?' Her green eyes were hopeful.

'I doubt it.' Jase shrugged his powerful shoulders. There was something inevitable in his words, and Lexa frowned.

'What was it about, anyway?'

'I'd have thought that was perfectly obvious.' His eyes mocked her gently and she flushed.

'There must have been more to it than ... than that. Nick wouldn't care if you ... if you. ...'

'Perhaps you underestimate the depth of Nick's feelings for you.'

'Don't play games with me, Jase, please!' She suddenly felt close to tears. Why did everything have to be so complicated, and what on earth was he getting at?

Jase crouched beside her and reaching out his hand, ran a long forefinger softly down her cheek.

'No games, Lexa, I'm deadly serious.'

'I don't believe you. Nick doesn't ... he isn't. ...' She swallowed painfully. 'Why do you say such things?' She was fighting, tears against anger, and her anger won. 'You shouldn't have hit him, you're much stronger than he is. It was all so stupid! You're brothers, doesn't that mean anything? I wish I'd never come home, I was better off in Switzerland. I wish I'd stayed there!' All her anger and hurt and frustration poured out in her words, a torrent of accusations against Jase.

His mouth tightened, his eyes becoming curiously blank as she shouted, letting her get it all out of her system. And when she had finished and was shaking uncontrollably, tears pouring down her face, he took her into his arms and held her tightly, not saying a word, but comforting her, rocking her gently until she quietened. Her tears had released all her anger, washing it away, and she lay still and silently in his arms knowing the bitter-sweet pain of his nearness.

It came to her then that there could never be anything permanent between Jase and herself. When he had kissed her, held her, when she had been thinking of him, she had been hoping, dreaming that he cared for her, not as his stepsister, a child to be indulged and treated kindly, but as a woman. I love him, she realised with a pang of despair. Perhaps it had been infatuation, a crush, when she first met him, but as she had grown up, got to know him better, her feelings had blossomed into love. Nobody would ever replace him in her heart, his strength, his gentleness, and those incredible golden eyes, they would haunt her for ever. There would never be anybody else.

She looked into his face, wondering how a love so strong could not be reciprocated. The events of the morning suddenly seemed petty, unimportant, nothing compared to her deep feelings. Nothing mattered except being with him like this.

'I'm sorry. I didn't mean those things I said and I didn't mean to cry all over you,' she said softly.

'That's okay—forget it.' He flashed her a brief smile. She reached up and traced the powerful contours of his face, answering some need deep within herself. Her mouth was dry, her throat aching as she touched him, her heart beginning to pound languorously. She felt him tense, and he caught her hand, stilling it against his cheek.

'Lexa, you don't know what you're doing to me,' he muttered roughly.

'I want you to kiss me,' she whispered, pressing her lips to his strong brown throat.

He framed her face with both his hands, staring at her with hungry intensity. 'How the hell can I resist you?' he murmured harshly. Her eyes were soft, luminous, her lips slightly parted, inviting his kiss. 'Oh, Lexa. . . .'

His mouth touched hers, brushing her lips with aching slowness, over and over, until she tangled her fingers in his dark hair, pulling him closer.

His kiss was an explosion, the passion flaring between them, catching them both unawares, the ferocity of it making them cling together. They were alone in the world, knowing only each other.

Lexa was completely lost as Jase's powerful arms tightened around her. His mouth searched hers deeply, exploring the inner sweetness of her lips, seeking, possessing, taking what she was desperately willing to give.

Her fingers were sliding beneath his shirt, stroking his warm, bare skin and her sweetly innocent caresses seemed to bring him suddenly to his senses. He released her abruptly, swinging away from her, moving swiftly, lithely to his feet.

Lexa watched through half-closed eyes as he put some distance between them. He was breathing heavily, his hands clenched into fists, the knuckles white with strain. He had his back to her, he was staring across the river, the set of his dark head proud and tense.

She felt dazed by what had happened between them, that sweet hungry passion that had flared out of control, dazed by Jase's sudden rejection of something they both knew they were powerless to resist.

She slowly got to her feet, a warm heat weakening her lower limbs, and walked towards him, sliding her arms around his waist from behind, pressing her body to the taut length of his back. 'Jase, hold me again,' she whispered, pressing her lips to his shoulder, sliding her fingers between the buttons of his shirt, touching the hard flatness of his stomach.

She heard him draw an uneven breath. 'Don't do that, Lexa,' he warned, in a low tense voice. 'Let me be.'

It was a painfully direct rejection and her arms stiffened, hurt and humiliation washing over her, as his words rang in her head. He wanted her, she would have staked her life on that knowledge, so why was he being so cruel?

'Have ... have I done something wrong?' she whispered, pain shaking her voice.

'Dammit, Lexa!' It was an explosion of anger. He turned on her, wrenching her arms from him, his eyes flaming dangerously out of control.

She stared at him, her mouth hurt and vulnerable. They were suddenly bitter enemies, a shocking desperate tension between them.

'Just drop it, will you?' he grated, his eyes burning her as they skimmed over her face.

'I want to know,' she persisted doggedly. 'What have I done to make you so angry? You want me——'

'I did want you,' he cut in, correcting her coldly. 'I don't want you now, got it?'

Lexa glared at him open-mouthed, deeply shocked by his callous words. Then anger rose, almost choking her, the other emotions inside her building up and building up, breaking her self-control.

'Nick was right,' she almost screamed at him. 'You are a bastard! I hate you!'

Jase's eyes glittered dangerously. He reached out, roughly grasping a handful of her soft curls, wrenching back her head, uncaring that he hurt her, his mouth a hard cruel line. He was as angry as she was, that violent tension almost unbearable, crackling like electricity between them. He swore long and hard, and Lexa, suddenly frightened of this furious, powerful man, whom she had pushed over the edge of control, tore herself away from him, gasping with pain as her hair was nearly pulled from its roots. She hated him! Her hate was fire inside her, all-consuming. It was too dangerous to stay. The air was full of savagery, awareness, emotion. She turned and ran, moving faster than she had ever done before in her life, but she only managed five yards before Jase caught her, pulling her round to face him.

'Let me go!' she demanded, her breath coming quickly.

'Never!' he gritted furiously.

Lexa hit out at him, beyond words now, her nails clawing for his face, her feet kicking for his shins, using her whole body to try and unbalance him. His hands were hurting her, bruising her arms and shoulders, both of them driven by something primitive and powerful, so strong that they could not fight it.

Using his superior strength, Jase pinned her hands behind her back, and she struggled impotently, suddenly remembering something Nick had taught her, classic self-defence. She entwined her legs with his and used the weight of her body to unbalance him. She heard him swear as they fell together, down on to the grass, and then Jase was arching over her, in control again, which wasn't the way it was supposed to happen, pinning her hands over her head, the weight of his body holding her still to the ground, his legs over hers. They were both breathing heavily, his glittering golden eyes skimming slowly over her, returning to her face, holding her gaze.

They stared at each other for immeasurable seconds and all the fury and all the anger was drained away, something fierce and primeval replacing it.

Lexa's heart was tripping over itself, hammering in her chest. There was fire in Jase's eyes. He bent his head very slowly and their mouths came together desperately, sweetly, fusing them with a fevered melting desire that shook them both.

He released her arms and they crept around his neck, his own hands sliding beneath her, holding her tightly, crushing her to the taut hardness of his body.

Then his mouth became gentle, brief. He raised his head, staring down at her. He smiled, a warm, charm-filled smile. He was totally in control of himself now, his potent attraction tearing at her heart.

He pushed the silk blouse from her slender shoulders, noticing the marks, soon to be bruises, made by his hands. He sighed, touching his mouth to her sore skin very tenderly. 'Did I do that? I'm sorry, my love,' he murmured against her throat.

'I bruise easily. It's not as bad as it looks.' Her voice was weak, her laugh shaky.

Jase moved lithely, rolling on to his back, his arms still round her.

'I always seem to end up playing the jealous adolescent when I'm with you,' he said wryly. 'I don't know why.' He stared up into the cloudles sky. Lexa knew what he was thinking. They were both shaken by what had just happened, the uncontrollable ferocity of it all. She still wanted him badly, she could tell by the tension in his body that he wanted her. She felt exhausted, drained, yet achingly alive.

Jase pulled a packet of cigarettes from his pocket. 'Want one?' He kissed her hair. She nodded and he lit two. She watched him smoke, her heart filled with intense pleasure. It was cool beneath the trees, the grass was soft. She wanted to sleep. She could hear the deep steady rhythm of Jase's heart beneath her cheek. She wanted to stay in this cool safe place for ever.

Jase was watching her, his eyes unfathomable, his fingers lightly stroking her arm. There was perfect communication between them, and as she knew his thoughts, he also knew what she was thinking.

'We should go back. Rex will be expecting us for lunch,' she said, unable to keep the regret out of her voice, as she glanced at the gold watch on his wrist.

'I guess so,' he said reluctantly. He kissed her mouth and with one graceful movement got to his feet, pulling her up with him.

Lexa smiled at him, unable to keep her heart out of her eyes. Jase slid his arm around her shoulders and they began to walk slowly back to the house.

CHAPTER FOUR

Lexa took a bath before she went to bed that night. She had the feeling that sleep was going to be elusive again.

She lay inert in the hot water. It had been quite a day and she felt exhausted, exhausted enough to go out like a light as soon as her head touched the pillow, yet her mind was buzzing, running in circles, denying her any rest.

There had been no sign of Nick at lunch and nobody had mentioned him. Marny had been out at work, which had left Rex, Jase and herself.

Rex had seemed a little subdued and Lexa had guessed that he was still a little upset about the fight. Jase had been charming, witty, talking to him about his work, chatting about his latest book, cheering him up. Lexa had watched him quietly as she ate, throwing the odd comment into the conversation now and again. She loved to hear Jase talk, he was clever, startling, so charming. It was no surprise to her that he had made his millions so young. She was desperately glad that they were on good terms again. Whenever Jase had looked at her, his eyes had been warm, gentle.

Late that afternoon, Zack Harvey had telephoned. Lexa had answered the phone herself, so there had been no escape. He had asked her out to the theatre, to the opening of a new play, the following week. She did not really want to go but had been unable to think of a single excuse. He had made her laugh, coaxing her to accept, and in the end she had given in, somehow admiring him for his persistence. He was a nice man, she had decided, as she replaced the receiver, but when she saw him, she would have to make it clear that there could only be friendship between them. After that, it would be up to him.

Dinner had been very strained. Jase was out—on business, Rex had said. Very opportune, Lexa thought, because Nick had still been in a foul mood.

Luckily, Marny had returned home early from work, so Lexa had had someone to talk to over the meal. Nick had eyed her sullenly from time to time and she had felt herself flushing under his cold scrutiny, hurt that he could be acting so childishly.

Rex and Marny had made a determined effort to lighten the heavy atmosphere, to cheer him up, all to no avail, and Lexa had breathed a sigh of relief when the meal was finally over and she had heard the roar of his car engine pulling down the drive.

Marny had left on a date about eight-thirty, Rex had disappeared into his study and Lexa had spent the rest of the evening watching television and making repairs to some of her clothes.

Despite her protests, Rex had given her an enormous sum of money for new clothes. She must go up to London, he had said, and re-stock her wardrobe. His tone had been final, brooking no argument.

Marny had been excited by the news. 'I'll come with you—it'll be great fun. I know all the best places.' So that had been settled for the end of the week when Marny had some time off.

Her life here was settling down, she thought, as she languidly soaped her shoulders. It was forming a very pleasant pattern. She was part of the family for sure; they had all been so kind to her.

She tried not to allow her thoughts to touch on Jase. Soon he would be flying back to New York. What would she do when he'd gone? She would be so empty, so lonely.

If she wanted to be near him then her only choice was to take the job he had offered her, and the thought of leaving Rex and Marny so soon made her feel decidedly miserable. She would not think about it until she had to. Jase would not be leaving for at least a week, probably longer.

As she shampooed her hair, she thought about what had happened between them by the river, the fierce hungry passion that had hit them both like a bomb, and it shocked her to her very soul—the anger, the tension, the realisation that she was in love with him, Jase's control, his withdrawal, when she would have given him everything. Something had happened, something pure and profound, and she would never forget it, even if she did not fully understand it.

There was a knocking on her door as she was drying her hair. 'Come in.' She carried on pulling the brush through her wet curls. It was Nick, walking uncertainly into the room, not quite looking her in the face. She switched off the hairdryer, looking at him warily.

'I want to talk to you,' he said uncomfortably.

'Sit down.' She gestured towards a low cane chair, wondering what on earth he wanted to talk about. She smiled at him. They were both nervous.

Nick pushed his long hair out of his face. Lexa noticed that his mouth was still a little swollen.

'What is it?' she asked gently.

'This morning—I was bloody rude to you—I'm sorry, Lexa.' He spoke quickly and she could see that he was very embarrassed.

'It doesn't matter, really it doesn't. I've forgotten about it.' She was generous, anxious to ease his embarrassment, to show him that everything was all right again.

'It does matter.' He stood up and walked restlessly over to the window.

Lexa watched him. He had that same unconscious grace that Jase had, his movements lithe and easy. He wasn't as tall as Jase, but his body was lean and muscular, with wide shoulders, narrow hips. He was very attractive, she realised, looking at him objectively for once, not comparing him to Jase. That was the trouble, she always compared the men she met with Jase. She always found them wanting.

Nick turned, his worried brown eyes meeting hers. 'I didn't mean what I said to you, it was unforgivable.'

'No, not unforgivable—please don't think that.' He was more distressed than she had realised and she honestly believed that what he had said did not matter. It was important that he believed her.

'Are we still friends?' he grinned crookedly.

Lexa smiled, holding out her hand. 'I hope so.'

Nick took her proffered hand, pulling her to her feet and hugging her, kissing her cheek. 'I've been feeling guilty all day. I thought I'd blown it for good with you.'

'No chance.'

'I'd like to explain——'

'There's no need.'

'I think there is—Lexa, I'm worried about you.'

'I don't want you to worry. I can look after myself,' she protested, beginning to feel uneasy.

'And Jase?'

She could feel herself blushing. 'What about Jase?'

'Well, for a start, just what is going on between you two?'

'Nick, I. . . .' She started to try and explain, but he cut across her.

'Let's face it, that was hardly a brotherly kiss I stumbled on this morning.' There was anger, raw and unleashed in his voice, suddenly burning in his face, his whole mood changing in a flash. For some reason, even the thought of Jase really got under his skin.

Lexa stared at him with hurt eyes. 'I don't see that it's any of your business,' she retorted, retaliating in the only way she could think of.

'No?' Nick was really angry now, his voice becoming louder. 'Let me tell you, you're making a big mistake if you get involved with him. Jase only means one thing, and that's trouble.'

'So that's my problem. Why should you care?' she protested, not wanting to fight with him.

Nick sighed, his shoulders suddenly hunching. 'I care about you,' he said quietly, his anger disappearing as quickly as it had flared up. 'You've no idea how much I care about you.'

Lexa turned away, fiddling nervously with the brush in her hand. 'What is it between you and Jase? What's happened to make everything so bitter between you?'

'Do you really want to know?' He was looking at her steadily, and there was pain in his eyes.

Lexa thought for a second. She had the feeling that Nick was about to tell her something dreadful. Did she really want to know?

'Yes, tell me,' she heard herself replying in an even voice.

Nick lit a cigarette, exhaling smoke slowly before he started speaking.

'You're right about this morning, there was more to it, although I can't deny I was angry to see you with him—like that.' He turned away, staring out of the window.

'Just over a year ago, I started seeing a girl—she sang with the band for a while, that's how we met. Her name was Eva, and like the fool I am, I fell in love with her and I fell hard. Everything was going fine, we were really close.' Nick's mouth twisted as his eyes met Lexa's again. 'That was, until she met Jase. He was over here on business. Eva came for a weekend.' He broke off, raking his hand through his hair.

'Oh, Nick, I'm so sorry! I . . . I don't know what to say.' Lexa bit her lip, hurting inside for him, almost wishing she had not asked him to tell her. She was not sure she wanted to know any more, but it was too late.

'You're not half as sorry as I am, believe me, and the best part is still to come. I watched her watching him all weekend, and they were the worst two days of my life. She couldn't drag her eyes away from him.' Nick swallowed convulsively, as though choking back some rough emotion that she could see in his eyes. 'What is it with him anyway?' he burst out, gazing relentlessly at Lexa, as though expecting some answer.

She lowered her eyes, her face bright with colour. What did he expect her to say? What could she say? She kept her eyes lowered in silence, until he started talking again.

'After that weekend, Eva changed, the bottom had fallen out of what we'd had together. She didn't even want to see me. I tried to find out if she was seeing Jase. He told me they weren't seeing each other, she told me they were—what the hell was I supposed to believe? I thought that when Jase went back to the States, it would fizzle out between them, then I could try again. But Jase didn't go back. Rex had that heart attack two weeks later, and Jase stayed. And so it went on, until one afternoon. . . . Well, I couldn't stand it any longer. I went to see Eva, to get the whole thing sorted out once and for all.' He paused, stubbing out his cigarette with careless fingers, his face twisted with pain. 'She told me that afternoon that she was pregnant and that she didn't want to see me again. Jase denied that he was the father, but dammit, she wasn't seeing anybody else!'

Lexa's eyes clouded over. Nick was obviously telling the truth, and she felt pain, clenching like a fist inside her.

'So what happened?' Some part of her, a terribly self-destructive part it seemed, was relentlessly forcing her to carry on asking questions.

Nick shrugged. 'I suppose Jase dumped her. He certainly took no responsibility for the child. I haven't seen Eva for nearly a year, she moved away soon after I saw her that afternoon and I couldn't trace her. I don't even know whether she's had the baby, although it was due a few months ago.'

'You still love her?' Lexa asked gently.

Nick nodded. 'I still love her,' he said flatly. 'Jase destroyed what we had together. He'll destroy you if you get involved with him.'

Lexa swallowed painfully. 'Doesn't Jase know where she is?'

'No, he says not. Anyway, what difference would it make, even if I could find her? She made it perfectly clear that as far as she was concerned, it was over between us. She laid it straight on the line. Lexa, leave Jase alone, don't get involved with him, please!' he begged, coming to crouch in front of her, taking both her hands in his.

Easier said than done, Lexa thought miserably; she was already totally and utterly involved with him. She loved him. Even Nick's story had not changed that.

'I'll do my best,' she lied, flashing him what she

hoped was a reassuring smile. 'And I don't want you to worry, Nick, I really can look after myself.'

'I thought Eva could look after herself. Jase is ruthless, destructive—I'll kill him if he hurts you!' Nick grated brutally, yet he seemed satisfied with her answer, because he got to his feet and managed a taut smile. 'Sorry to burden you with all this—I didn't mean to. And I am sorry about this morning.' He walked towards the door, pulling it open. 'Goodnight, love.'

'Goodnight, Nick.' Lexa could hardly speak, she felt so full of sorrow for him, so full of self-pity for herself. Had Jase really stolen the woman Nick loved, made her pregnant and then abandoned her? Was that what he had been trying to warn her about, the first night she came home? She couldn't believe that he would do something so callous, he would not treat people with such heartless disregard. Nick must have got it wrong. Her lips stretched into a bitter smile. She was defending him, even now she was defending him, and what did she really know of him? According to the newspapers, and that was all she had to go on, his affairs were many, his women beautiful, eager. Why shouldn't she believe Nick?

She sighed as she thought of her young stepbrother. He was tearing himself apart. He loved Jase, had always respected and admired him, had looked up to him as his elder brother, but Jase had stolen his lover, treated her shabbily, given her his child, then left her.

Nick's explosion that morning was suddenly very understandable, and she went to sleep feeling restless and troubled.

When she appeared for breakfast the next morning, lethargic and heavy-eyed, she found Rex and Jase in the dining room.

'Good morning, Lexa. Sleep well?' Rex smiled at her, as she entered the room.

She kissed his cheek. 'Morning, Rex, Jase.' She flashed Jase a quick glance, her heart turning over. This morning he was wearing a dark, finely pin-striped suit, the expensive material expertly tailored to his powerful body, and a pale grey shirt. He looked formal, remote, devastatingly attractive.

His eyes flicked over her impassively as he raised his head from the newspaper he was reading. 'Lexa,' he nodded, and immediately returned his attention to the paper. He was obviously in no mood to talk.

She poured herself some coffee and sat down next to Rex, buttering a thin slice of toast without enthusiasm. She didn't feel very hungry, but she could feel Rex's eyes on her, so she nibbled at it halfheartedly. 'Where is everybody?' she asked cheerfully.

'Marny left very early. I haven't seen Nick,' Rex replied. 'I suppose he's still in bed.'

Glancing up, Lexa found Jase's eyes upon her and realised that he was very angry. She caught her breath, confused and rather frightened, by the raw fury she saw in his face, her own eyes innocent, questioning.

What on earth was the matter with him? She lowered her eyes confusedly, and nervously sipped her coffee. He had obviously got out of bed on the wrong side.

'Any plans for today?' Rex's easy question cut into her troubled reverie.

'I'm going up to London to meet Marny for lunch.' She turned her attention to her stepfather, trying to ignore the savagely angry man sitting opposite her.

'That should be very pleasant, my dear,' Rex said vaguely, and she had the feeling that his thoughts were elsewhere. 'When are you going?'

'Right after breakfast. I thought I might do some shopping. There's a train in forty minutes.' She glanced at her watch. 'Goodness, I'd better hurry!'

'Jase is driving up to London directly after breakfast. I'm sure he'll give you a lift. Jase?'

'No, no. Really . . . I'd rather. . . .' Lexa stammered hurriedly. She did not want to spend time with Jase when he was so obviously in a rotten mood. Her instincts were telling her that his fury was, for some inexplicable reason, directed against her.

'I'll be glad to,' Jase cut in smoothly, his eyes telling her that he would not be glad at all.

'Good, that's settled. So much more comfortable than the train.' Rex smiled, seemingly unaware of the undercurrents around the table.

'Yes, thank you.' Lexa had the feeling that she had been backed into a corner.

Jase rose to his feet, throwing back his coffee in two long mouthfuls. 'I'll see you outside in twenty minutes,' he said expressionlessly. Lexa knew that he was looking at her, but did not raise her head. 'Okay,' she replied, falsely cheerful, sighing with relief as he left the room. She only hoped that he would be in a better mood on the journey. He had already successfully ruined her breakfast without even trying.

'More coffee?' she asked Rex as she poured out some more for herself.

'Mm? Oh, yes—thank you, my dear.'

'You're in a very thoughtful mood,' she teased him, adding milk to her cup.

'Forgive me,' he said graciously. 'I've hit a particularly sticky patch in this book I'm working on at the moment, and I can't seem to get my mind off it.'

Lexa smiled, watching him affectionately. He was a wonderful man, mellowing as the years passed, his lightning, fearful tempers becoming fewer and fewer. His vagueness concealed the strong, forceful personality that had held the rambling family together, over the years.

He had been so kind to her, so generous, she would never be able to repay him. She did not even know where to begin.

'Jase seems bad-tempered this morning,' she remarked, glancing at her watch again. She did not dare to be late.

'He has a lot on his mind, I suppose,' said Rex, eyeing her shrewdly. 'He works hard, and he's a remarkable man, he's strong, twice as strong as I ever was, and self-contained. He's difficult to read, yes, but look beneath that cool, sophisticated shell and you find a warm, brilliant mind, a very generous heart and the gentleness of the truly strong. He's a very complex man.' Her stepfather spoke with slow pride. 'And he's very fond of you, Lexa. Try to see beneath his abruptness, his anger—none of it matters and you shouldn't let it hurt you.'

He was very serious, telling her something important, and she listened carefully, not surprised by his perception of Jase and of herself.

'I'll try,' she promised gently. She had glimpsed Jase's warmth, his tenderness, and it bound her to him more securely than iron chains. Was he fond of her? She wanted more, she wanted everything.

'Thank you.' She squeezed Rex's arm, understanding what he was trying to tell her. 'I'd better go. Can I fetch you anything from town?'

'I don't think so. Enjoy yourself.'

'I will. 'Bye!' She hurried from the room, colliding with Nick in the doorway.

'Hey, where's the fire?' He steadied her easily, his eyes friendly but slightly guarded. They were both thinking about the night before.

'Sorry, Nick—Jase is waiting for me.' She did not mistake the slight tightening of his mouth, but she ignored it, smiling up into his face.

He released her without a word and she ran nimbly upstairs to collect her jacket and handbag. The situation was becoming impossible! She was caught in the middle of this bitterness between Jase and Nick, being pulled two ways all the time. But what could she do?

She shrugged into her jacket and brushed her hair. She was already three minutes late. Grabbing her bag, she ran down the stairs like the wind and outside into the sunlight of another beautiful day.

Jase was leaning indolently against the black Mercedes. His eyes moved over her in slow appraisal as she arrived by his side, taking in her fashionably loose russet trousers, her cream silk blouse, her matching jacket and gold jewellery, her stunning, breathless beauty. The sun was shining in her hair, turning it into a spun gold halo around her pointed face.

'I'm sorry. . . .' she began, catching her breath, fearful that he was about to tell her off.

'Get in.' He ignored her apology, holding open the passenger door for her. His mood had not improved, Lexa thought wryly, as she slid inside the car.

The leather upholstery was soft to her touch, the windows slightly tinted, reducing the glare of the sun. It was wonderfully comfortable. As Rex had pointed out, much more comfortable than the train.

Jase slid in beside her, seconds later. He was silent. The engine roared into life, the car shooting smoothly down the drive, in a spray of gravel.

Lexa curled herself up against the door, as far away as she could get from him. His anger was threatening, almost tangible in the expensive confines of the car. She felt compelled to say something, anything to break the silence.

'You don't have to give me a lift,' she began nervously, as the car pulled speedily on to the road. 'You could drop me at the station.' And when he was still silent, she added, 'I know Rex kind of forced you into it.'

Without looking at her, Jase said coldly, 'Don't be ridiculous. I'm driving into the City anyway, and Rex couldn't force me to do anything I didn't want to do.'

Lexa bit her lip, hurt by the ice in his voice, and tried to squeeze herself even further into the corner, away from him. Something had changed, but infuriatingly, she did not know what. Everything had been so beautiful between them yesterday, but now it seemed that had all gone. Today Jase was a stranger, a cold, hard stranger.

She glanced covertly at his profile. It was closed, totally expressionless. She stared at his hands on the wheel, controlling the powerful vehicle with effortless ease. They were strong, tanned, with long hard fingers. She fought the ache of desire that rose in her as she looked at those hands. Jase was an expert lover, of that she had no doubt, even though she had little experience. He could arouse her so easily, without even trying, she thought bitterly.

They were picking up speed now, the car purring, eating up the miles. Lexa shifted restlessly, squashed by the ominous atmosphere between them.

Jase lit a thin cheroot, the smoke curling from his firm mouth. He had not said a word.

'Why are you so angry this morning?' she asked at last, cursing her voice for sounding so small and frightened. She had to ask, though. Jase might be able to stand this awful tension, but it was getting to her. She could not bear it.

His eyes left the road for a second, meeting hers, the

golden depths hard and blank. 'Now why do you think?' he drawled with cold mockery.

Lexa sighed. 'I wouldn't be asking if I knew, would I?'

The powerful shoulders lifted. 'How should I know?' There was a wealth of meaning in his voice.

'Because I tell you. Have I done something wrong?' She begged for his kindness. She hated herself for doing it, but could not help it.

'You obviously don't think so, but how about dropping the injured innocence?' His mouth twisted cynically, and Lexa felt a rush of tears scalding her eyelids.

'What have I done? Please—tell me!'

She saw his jaw clench, a muscle jerking in his face.

'Let's talk about last night, shall we?'

Lexa stared at him blankly. 'What about last night?'

She had no idea what he was talking about. He hadn't even been there. The only thing of importance that had happened last night had been her talk with Nick. Had Jase overheard something? It was the only thing she could think of, and Jase's proud, cold face told her that he was not going to give her any help.

'This wouldn't have anything to do with Nick, by any chance?' she asked coldly. Had Jase been eavesdropping?

'It sure as hell would!' he bit out furiously. 'You ought to be damned glad that it was me who caught him creeping out of your bedroom after midnight, and not Rex!'

Realisation dawned with his words, and her outrage that he should have made such assumptions about her and Nick was tinged with hysterical amusement at the sheer ridiculousness of the very idea. *Her and Nick?*

She couldn't help it. The laughter was bubbling in her

throat, out of her mouth, high and clear, filling the car, falling around them both, into the anger and the tension. She saw Jase's hands clenching on the wheel, his face tightening and she heard him swear violently.

'I'm glad you find it so amusing. I doubt Rex would have taken the same attitude.' His voice was low, very ominous.

'You think that Nick and I . . .?' Lexa's voice broke and she dissolved into helpless giggles. She knew it was unwise, that it only angered Jase even more, but she was powerless to stop.

She was totally, utterly involved with Jase. She couldn't even look at another man. How could he not know that? How could he even begin to imagine her with Nick?

The car swerved to a sudden violent halt, and Jase turned to her, his eyes shooting fire. 'I don't think, you little bitch,' he grated coldly, 'I bloody know!' His hands closed on her shoulders, their grip punishing, bruising.

Her smile was tinged with fear. One look into his fierce golden eyes stopped her hysteria in its tracks. 'You can't know. . . .' she began quietly, frightened now, feeling as though she was trapped in some dark nightmare.

'That's what you'd like to think—hard luck, sweetheart. Believe me, I know.' His glittering gaze moved to her parted lips. She pushed futilely at his wide, unyielding shoulders, understanding that look in his eyes. 'No, Jase, don't. . . .' she pleaded, knowing that he would hurt her.

'You give yourself freely, Lexa. I've tasted the innocence of your mouth, and I want more—I want what I lie awake at nights aching for, I want what you give to Nick,' he said very slowly, very coldly.

One hand slid along the slender column of her neck, up to tangle in her hair, pulling back her head, exposing her mouth, her throat. His warm angry mouth gently touched her throat and she quivered beneath his hands.

She heard him laugh, deeply, humourlessly, his lips trailing like fire over her skin. But the mouth that possessed hers, seconds later, was not gentle, it was brutal, punishing, grinding her lips against her teeth as Jase purged his fury on her.

Lexa twisted beneath that cruel mouth, more angry with herself than with him, because deep inside her she could feel an unbidden response rising. A response that made her *ache* to touch his thick black hair, his smooth skin, to kiss him back, to coax away his anger with sweet yielding passion. Yet if she did that, if she responded in any way at all to the cynical mouth that moved on hers, he would think the worst of her. For him it would prove what he thought about her and Nick, and she hated him for that.

She stiffened her lips until they were numb, fighting the hardest battle of her life, refusing to allow Jase the triumph of the tiniest response. And when she thought she was losing that battle, she tore herself away from him, uncaring of the physical pain, crying out as she fought his immense strength, staring at him with wide hurt eyes, moving away until her back was in contact with the coolness of the car door.

As though regretting what he had done, surprised by her resistance, Jase let her go easily, not attempting to touch her again, though his eyes were still angry, contemptuous as they rested on her swollen mouth. Her lips were throbbing and she touched them tentatively with her fingers. 'You hurt me,' she whispered miserably, shocked by his actions, his fury.

'That's nothing to what I'd like to do to you,' he

muttered savagely. 'I swear, I'd like to kill you—and him! This is some bloody revenge he's thought up! The only trouble is that it'll hurt Rex one hell of a sight more than it'll hurt me. I don't suppose you even thought about that last night.'

He was attacking her fiercely, without remorse, so damned sure that he was right, and she felt bruised, hurt, with only her anger at his injustice to fight back with.

'You've got it all wrong——' she began heatedly.

'On the contrary, perhaps I'm seeing you clearly for the first time,' he drawled hatefully.

'Please, Jase, listen to me! Why should you think that Nick and I . . . that we . . .?' She couldn't say the words, flushing hotly beneath his savagely relentless gaze.

Jase's mouth twisted in the semblance of a bitter smile. 'That you're lovers?' he supplied harshly. 'It isn't something I've dreamed up myself. Nick admitted it to me, so you can drop this ridiculous pretence, Lexa, my love. I know everything but the sordid details.'

Lexa was stunned. 'Nick admitted it?' she echoed confusedly, unaware that her faltering question would be taken by Jase as a damning admission of guilt.

'You certainly can't rely on his discretion.' That cold, hard mockery was back, taunting and disdainful. She grabbed at his arm, the fine expensive material of his jacket sliding beneath her desperate fingertips, sliding like all her dreams. She *had* to convince him that Nick had been lying.

'It's not true—believe me, Jase, it's not true!' she protested fiercely, willing him to believe her.

'No?' His voice was flat, almost uninterested, belied by that strange blank savagery that glittered in the golden depths of his eyes. 'And why shouldn't I believe him? I caught him coming from your room, he admitted it to me, face to face, and I know he's been watching you like a hawk ever since you got back—I even saw him kissing you the day you arrived! So give me one good reason why I shouldn't believe him. No wonder he was so angry at the pool the other morning!'

Lexa was suddenly defeated, broken by his anger, by Nick's lies.

'I have no good reasons,' she said huskily. 'I can only tell you that it's not true.'

Jase laughed, an icy, ugly sound. 'So sweet, so innocent—I could almost be taken in by you, if I didn't know better,' he drawled cynically. 'But let me tell you, if Rex finds out about this, you're going to wish you'd never been born! Got that? You might relay that message to your lover as well, it also goes for him!'

He switched on the engine, signifying that as far as he was concerned, the conversation was at an end.

The car screeched protestingly back on to the road, speeding up at an almost frightening pace, but Lexa did not even notice.

'I'd never hurt Rex,' she said numbly, staring at Jase's stone-hard profile.

'I'm glad to hear that you still have one or two scruples left,' he retorted with heavy sarcasm. He did not even look at her. Lexa watched the muscle jerking spasmodically in his jaw, with dull eyes. She had tried to convince him and failed. He would never believe her—never. He believed his brother, she couldn't blame him for that, she couldn't even feel angry with Nick, only sorry for him, hurt that he had involved her even further in his bitter battle with Jase.

As Jase had said, it was revenge, and Lexa was a useful pawn. The trouble was that if Nick's lies were made public, then Rex would be hurt.

How could Nick have said such things? she wondered miserably, but deep in her heart, she knew. Nick knew that Jase wanted her, he had seen it with his own eyes that morning by the pool when they had fought. He had told Jase that he and Lexa had become lovers, knowing that Jase would be violently angry, knowing that Jase would say nothing for fear of hurting Rex.

Cleverly contained and guaranteed to cause one hell of a lot of trouble. And all because Nick had lost the woman he loved to Jase!

They were intent on destroying each other, it seemed, and Nick's bitterness was a dangerous force. He was so bitter, so intent on hitting back at his brother that he did not care that Lexa was being badly hurt in the process. He had no idea how much damage he had done, she thought, feeling a bitterness of her own welling up in her heart.

Jase hated her now, and nothing could change the way he saw her. She was deeply in love with a man who couldn't stand the sight of her. In his eyes, she was cheap, immoral, uncaring of other people's feelings.

The fact that she responded so passionately, so lovingly to him, only fuelled his contemptuous opinion of her, his belief in her easy virtue. Nick had destroyed any caring for her in Jase. He had been trying to destroy his brother, but he had only succeeded in destroying Lexa's dreams for the future, and she had never before felt so helpless or so miserable.

CHAPTER FIVE

LUNCH with Marny was an absolute disaster, Lexa felt numb, dead inside; she seemed to be functioning on automatic.

Marny was very bright, excited about a new job she had just that morning landed, and she chattered merrily, nineteen to the dozen. Then at last she noticed Lexa's trance-like misery, asking what was wrong, and Lexa pleaded a splitting headache so convincingly that Marny believed her. Lexa listened to what Marny was saying with a tiny portion of her mind, amazed that she could answer, talk almost normally, when her heart felt as though it was breaking.

She went over and over what Jase had said, convinced that she would never be able to make him change his mind. She was doomed, she thought miserably, eating the grapes on the plate in front of her without even noticing.

Marny had an appointment at two, so when they split up outside the restaurant, with Lexa apologising profusely for her mood over the meal, she decided to go straight home. She had no enthusiasm for trailing round the shops. She had no enthusiasm for anything after this morning. She caught the train and a bus and arrived home late in the afternoon. She went straight up to her room and took a cool shower, glad to wash away the dirt of the city. Then she lay on her bed, and for the first time since Jase had spoken to her so cruelly, allowed herself to cry, releasing some of the anger, the pain and bitterness inside her.

She felt so vulnerable, as though she had been skinned alive, weighed down with the misery of Jase's contempt. And worst of all was the fact that there was nothing at all she could do, only let her pride rescue her, try to pretend to the outside world in general, and Jase in particular, that she did not give a damn what anybody thought. It seemed the only way she could survive, to split her personality in two, the desperately hurt side to be hidden, the hard uncaring side, shown to the world.

She dried her face, splashing her red eyes with cold water, then, smoothing down her white sundress, went downstairs in search of a cold drink. She suddenly felt very thirsty.

The house was deserted. Mrs Frone had taken three days off to visit her ailing sister and Lexa found a note from Rex explaining that he had gone to visit a friend.

It was Lexa's turn to cook dinner that night in the absence of Mrs Frone, Marny's the following night. She wandered into the kitchen and poured herself a glass of milk from the refrigerator, and thought about what she would prepare for the evening meal. She enjoyed cooking and at least it would take her mind off Jase.

Would he be in for dinner? She hoped not. She did not know how she was going to face him. She closed her eyes and pressed a hand to her throat. She could not block what he had said out of her mind. How could he have done such a thing!

She washed the glass she had been drinking from, carelessly placing it on the draining board.

In the refrigerator she found that Mrs Frone had left a leg of cold stuffed lamb. It was marked on the copious instructions she had also left, as being earmarked for that day. They would have that for dinner, she thought purposefully. She would prepare rice salad and green salad and serve them with brown bread, then fresh strawberries and cheese for dessert. That was sorted out.

She wandered upstairs again, hearing Nick at the piano in the lounge. Resolve stiffened her spine as she moved towards the lounge door. It was time to have it out with him for what he had done.

She strolled into the room, hoping that she looked calm, nonchalant. Nick looked up as she entered, his fingers hovering over the piano keys, the music stopping abruptly.

'Hi, you're back early,' he smiled easily.

'Shopping didn't appeal to me,' she replied casually, curling herself up on a velvet-covered chair near the open windows, scratching the head of one of the dogs who came and thrust his nose into her lap. Nick was acting normally. Did he think that she did not know what he had said?

'Enjoy your lunch?' He was flicking through a pile of sheet music.

'Yes, it was great. Marny's just landed a new contract. She'll probably tell you all about it herself over dinner.'

Lexa stared at her stepbrother. It came to her then that she hardly knew him. She had no idea what made him tick, the ins and outs of his personality. She knew only the surface image, the warm friendly man who was projected on the outside world.

She fell silent, and as the minutes ticked by, it became obvious that he was not going to mention his lies to Jase, even though she was giving him every opportunity to do so. He was seemingly engrossed in his work and it looked as though she would have to broach the subject herself. She took a deep breath.

'Why did you tell Jase that you and I have become

lovers?' she asked quietly and directly, amazed that she sounded so cool when the words hurt her so much to say.

Nick's head shot up and his eyes met hers uneasily, defiantly. Their glances held, Lexa's eyes cool and innocent, and a dull red flush crept along the line of his cheekbones, as he broke the contact first.

'He told you, then?' His voice was barely a mumble.

She nodded. 'In the car, this morning, in very graphic detail.' She paused, staring at him relentlessly. 'Why did you do it?'

'Does it make a difference?' Nick asked sullenly.

'Of course it does! What sort of a position do you think it puts me in with Jase?' she demanded, feeling her coolness disolving, her anger rising. He did not seem in the least regretful.

'At least it will keep him away from you,' said Nick with faint satisfaction, running a hand through his dark hair.

'And what gave you the right to make that sort of decision for me? If I want Jase to stay away from me, I can handle it myself, in my own way. I don't need you stepping in and telling lies!' She was really angry now. Nick honestly thought he had done the right thing, done her a favour! She could hardly believe it.

'I didn't think you could handle it on your own,' he muttered defensively.

'How can you be so arrogant!' Lexa gasped, her colour rising. 'If you're trying to tell me that you told Jase a pack of lies, just to protect me from him. . . .'

'How the hell was I supposed to know he was going to confront you with it?' Nick cut in, angry himself suddenly.

'Oh, I see. You had no intention of telling me

yourself. It was all planned to go on behind my back,' she retorted angrily.

'Look, I thought you needed to be protected from him. I thought he would just leave you alone and that would be the end of it.' Nick glanced at her quickly, then his eyes shifted restlessly away.

'Well, I'm glad he did tell me, glad that I've found you out!'

'Lexa, I was only thinking of you—you didn't seem able to handle him. . . .'

'How dare you! I'm not a child, I'm twenty years old, perfectly capable of sorting out my own life. Whether or not I can handle Jase is *my* business, and you had no right to interfere,' she said fiercely, hating him for being so patronising. 'If you *really* had my best interest at heart, why didn't you come to me and tell me what you intended to do?'

'You wouldn't have agreed to it,' Nick replied flatly.

'You're dead right, I wouldn't! You knew that, yet you still went ahead and did it. Would *you* like somebody telling lies about you behind your back, *supposedly* for your own good? Would you?' she demanded, glaring at him, her temper well and truly lost.

Nick lit a cigarette and regarded her through a haze of smoke, his eyes hard. 'You're blowing this up out of all proportion,' he told her casually. 'When you calm down and think about it rationally——'

'Oh!' She could hardly bear to listen to him. She felt like beating him to a pulp. 'You infuriating swine!'

It was on the tip of her tongue to tell him exactly what he had done, what damage he had caused, but she bit the words back just in time. She could not trust Nick with the knowledge of her love for Jase.

'You're not in the least bit sorry, are you?' she queried amazedly.

'I thought I was doing the right thing for you. I don't want you ending up like Eva,' came the stolidly-spoken reply. 'I don't want Jase hurting you the way he hurt her.'

'I wondered when Eva's name would be brought into it. Let's face it, it's Eva at the bottom of all this, isn't it?' Lexa said unsteadily. 'It's got nothing to do with me at all, you're just using me to get back at Jase for what he did to Eva, what he did to you.'

Nick's shoulders hunched, he suddenly seemed to shrink, his face becoming haunted as her words sank in.

'Maybe you're right. Maybe I did want to snatch something Jase wanted from under his nose, the way he snatched Eva,' he admitted heavily, after a long pause. 'And make no mistake, he wanted you. I thought he was going to kill me last night when he caught me coming from your room! It wasn't planned, I swear it wasn't. He had me pinned against the wall. I was helpless, I couldn't get away from him. I saw it in his eyes, the suspicion, the anger. He handed it to me on a plate . . . I just made it up on the spot.' He sighed, and although Lexa searched his face carefully, she could see no sign of triumph at his success. 'I'm sorry, Lexa, you've been right all along, of course. But it really did happen on the spur of the moment, Jase believed me and there was no going back after that.'

She felt the tears flooding into her eyes. There *was* no going back, that was the trouble. She did not feel angry any more. What was the point?

Nick's anger, his arrogance had all been guilt and immaturity, and he was ashamed of what he had done. Lexa wanted to ask him to go to Jase, tell him the truth, but she stopped herself. Jase would not believe it. It was too late. He would merely think that both she and Nick had been frightened by his anger, his threats. The evidence was weighed too heavily against them, and everything was lost.

'I just wish you hadn't done it,' she said wistfully, uselessly.

'I *know* I shouldn't have done it. I'm sorry.' He looked at her hopefully. Lexa saw that hope and turned away. He was waiting for her to say that everything was all right between them, but she found that she couldn't.

Nick's actions, whatever the motives behind them, had betrayed her, used her, and she could not forget that. She could not look at him as a friend, not yet anyway. Perhaps in a little while, when she had got over it. Despair rose in her. If she ever did get over it.

Nick hadn't known, of course, how she loved Jase, wanted him more than he had ever wanted her, so it had not been totally calculated to hurt, but the damage had been done nonetheless, and Nick was responsible.

She remembered something then. 'Jase mentioned Rex,' she said flatly. 'He said that Rex mustn't find out, and I agreed.'

Nick nodded. 'Something else I hadn't thought of. Dammit, why didn't Jase keep quiet!'

'I'm glad he didn't,' said Lexa with tired dignity. She got to her feet, not wanting to talk any more. 'I'll see you later. Will you be here for dinner? It's my turn to cook and I need to know how many there'll be.'

'No way,' Nick replied grimly. 'I'm keeping out of Jase's way. I'm going to a concert anyway, so don't bother about me.'

'Right.' She did not look back as she left the room, even though she knew that Nick was staring at her, willing her to say something else.

She heard the crash of his hands on the piano keys, without concern. His guilt was his own problem and she had no comfort left for him.

As she set the table for dinner, setting for four, even though she didn't know whether Jase would be in, she began to think seriously about her future, a future that stretched ahead of her, desperately empty. She knew that she could not put it off for much longer.

Jase's offer of a job she took as withdrawn after this morning. It would be impossible working for him now. So what would she do?

The atmosphere in the house was lethal at the moment, but Jase would be going back to New York fairly soon and if she kept out of Nick's way for a while, life here would be bearable, she decided, not wanting to leave Marny or Rex. Which left the problem of a job. She would begin looking tomorrow. It would get her out of the house and, with luck, stop her brooding.

Deep in thought, she did not notice the door swinging open behind her, but as though sensing somebody watching her, she turned suddenly to find Jase leaning indolently against the door-jamb staring at her as she worked, his face a cool expressionless mask.

She flushed deeply, turning back to her work, her heart beating so fast she thought it might burst.

Silence stretched between them, and her fingers became clumsy, nervous, she was dropping cutlery, almost breaking a plate, and she could feel his eyes on her, almost tangible in their probing.

She took a deep breath, trying to pull herself together, determined that he would not see how he unnerved her. With the table finished, she turned to him with a wary smile, her eyes flicking over him hungrily.

His jacket was slung on one finger over his shoulder, waistcoat open, tie discarded, his shirt open low at the neck, the skin beneath smooth and tanned. He looked tired, lines of strain around his firm, beautiful mouth, and her heart went out to him.

'I'm just about to make some coffee,' she said nervously. 'Would you like some?' Her green eyes beseeched him, begging for peace between them.

At first she thought he was going to ignore her question. He continued staring at her, noting the tense movements of her hands, the white teeth sunk into her bottom lip, the sad pleading beauty of her eyes.

Then he nodded. 'I could surely use a cup of coffee,' he said with a slight smile. He ran a hand tiredly around the back of his neck, drawing Lexa's attention to the powerful muscles of his shoulders beneath the fine silken material of his shirt. 'It's been one hell of a day.'

Lexa knew exactly what he meant, and she smiled as she moved past him to go to the kitchen.

Jase did not move and for a few seconds they were very close, their bodies almost touching in the doorway. Lexa was holding her breath, she realised. She could feel the warmth of his body and glancing up into his lean face, saw a dark flaming heat in his golden eyes before the shutters dropped and they were totally blank again.

She moved out into the hall and walked towards the kitchen on legs that felt like jelly, desperately aware that he was right behind her.

She made the coffee as quickly as she could and Jase sat on the edge of the table, idly smoking, watching her.

She poured out two cups as soon as it was ready and handed one to him, drawing her trembling fingers away quickly as though burned, not missing his cynical smile.

'Will . . . will you be in for dinner?' she asked in a small voice, drinking her coffee scalding hot. She longed to stay with him, yet she needed to get away. It was a strange feeling and one that she could not properly cope with.

Jase nodded. 'Yes. Why do you ask?'

'I'm cooking,' she explained with a sweet smile.

His eyes narrowed sharply on her face. 'Have you told Nick to keep his mouth shut?' he demanded, suddenly harsh.

Pain flashed through her. She felt as though she was being torn up inside. 'Yes, I told him,' she replied very quietly. She *had* to have one last try. Lifting her head, she looked him straight in the eye, inwardly quaking at what she saw in his expression. 'It's not true, you know. Nick and I are not lovers,' she said slowly.

Something froze behind Jase's eyes. He caught her chin in his hard fingers, holding her head still as he searched her face. His touch weakened her, his cool fingers like fire against her skin.

'Why are you trying so hard to convince me?' he queried softly, his fingers moving seemingly of their own volition over the rounded softness of her jaw.

'I want you to know the truth,' she whispered, deeply affected by his nearness, his touch on her skin.

'The truth.' He echoed her words slowly, curiously, as though they were in some foreign language that he had never heard before. 'Do you think I care whether or not you're sleeping with my brother?' There was a rough edge of violence in his voice. 'Do you think it matters to me, my love?'

Lexa's confusion was mirrored in her wide innocent eyes. She stared at the hard line of his mouth. 'Jase, please. . . .' She was frightened, of what, she did not know—something in his face, something in his voice.

'Please, what? What do you want of me, Lexa? Approval? Do you expect me to condone this sordid affair? You know damn well that you're playing with fire.'

'But it's not true!' she burst out, trembling beneath his hand.

He felt the tremor that ran through her, and his fingers became curiously gentle as they traced the vulnerable line of her mouth.

'So why the hell don't I believe you?' His hand dropped abruptly. Perhaps he could not bear to touch her any more, she thought painfully.

'I don't know.' Her words were heavy with defeat.

Jase sighed deeply, moving to his feet. 'Neither do I,' he said savagely, then walked from the room in silence.

A week later, Lexa went to the theatre with Zack Harvey.

As she made up her face at her dressing table mirror, she wondered why on earth she had agreed to go. Then she remembered his gentle humour, the way he had made her laugh while persuading her to accept his invitation.

It would be good to have some friendly uncomplicated company for the evening; she was feeling weighed down by the tense undercurrents in the house.

During the past week, she had not seen Jase alone, a fact about which she had mixed feelings, relief and sadness. When they were together in company, he was coolly polite, treating her as though she was a stranger, watching her like a hawk whenever she was in the same room as Nick.

Rex, vague and still heavily involved with his latest book, seemed to have noticed nothing wrong, but Marny had picked up on it the very first day.

'What on earth's the matter with Jase?' she had asked Lexa, with a certain amount of irritation. 'Have you two fallen out? You could have cut the atmosphere with a knife over dinner!'

Lexa had shrugged. 'Maybe he's overworking,' she had replied with careful disinterest. 'Who knows?' Marny had flashed her a searching look and had been forced to drop the subject.

Lexa was giving nothing away, even though it was an uphill struggle to keep her emotions under cool control. She usually cried at night in the privacy of her own room, which afforded her some release.

Jase's attitude hurt her so much and the strain was beginning to tell, she realised, tracing the dark circles beneath her eyes, quickly covering them with concealing make-up.

Nick had been keeping out of her way as well. She had only seen him at mealtimes, never alone, which suited her fine, as she could still not bring herself to feel kindly disposed towards him.

Every time she looked at him, she felt angry, her anger tempered with a wistful sorrow, a strange compassion. He would have been insulted by her pity, though, so it was better that they did not spend much time together.

Lexa also felt guilty. She felt as though she had split the family down the middle. None of it would have happened if she had not come back from Switzerland, she thought, with a hollow self-pity.

And the fact that she had nobody to really confide in made it all the more difficult to bear. She couldn't talk to Rex or Marny and all her closest friends from college were either still in Switzerland or on holiday abroad.

With a deep sigh, she slipped into the dress she had chosen for the evening. It was black silk with heavy ruffles around the neckline and hem. It was part of her new wardrobe, paid for by Rex, chosen with Marny's help.

It looked good on her, she thought without pleasure,

as she twirled in front of the mirror, the stark colour giving her hair the sheen of white gold, accentuating the brilliant emerald of her eyes. She clipped on a thin diamond necklace and slid her feet into high-heeled black shoes. She was ready and Zack would be arriving in five minutes. Collecting a shawl and her handbag, she switched off the light over her dressing table and left the room. Unfortunately she noticed Jase stepping out on to the wide landing at the same time as she shut the door. The noise turned his head round and it was too late to duck back inside.

He waited for her to catch up with him, his narrowed eyes sliding from the top of her golden head to her slim ankles, in slow expressionless appraisal.

Lexa watched him too, her eyes drawn hungrily to his wide shoulders beneath the maroon velvet of his dinner jacket. His hard-boned face was freshly shaven, smooth, his black hair faintly damp from the shower. He looked powerful, sophisticated, potently attractive, and she wished with all her heart that she was spending the evening with him.

She had imagined it so many times when she was alone. In her dreams, Jase was never angry or contemptuous, he cared for her, was warm and charming, both of them fiercely happy in each other's company. She blocked those sweet thoughts from her mind now as she reached his side, and her stomach tightened in reaction to his breathtaking magnetism.

'Beautiful,' he murmured, his mouth twisting. 'Quite beautiful. Nick is in for a very pleasant surprise.'

'I'll take that as a compliment, although I'm sure you didn't mean it to be one,' she said coolly, not meeting his eye.

They walked side by side down the stairs. 'And for your information, I don't suppose I'll even be seeing

Nick tonight,' she told him, pulling a face at his hard profile.

Jase's dark brows rose. 'Oh? So who will be having the pleasure of your—er—company tonight?' he asked softly.

'I'm going to the theatre with Zack Harvey,' she revealed airily, the insinuation in his last remark not lost on her.

His jaw tightened. 'My, you do get around, don't you?'

Before she had time to reply, he was striding away from her and she heard the roar of his car engine moments later, feeling weak with relief that she had not revealed anything of her feelings, of her hurt, to him. Who would he be dining with tonight? she wondered painfully, as the doorbell clanged. Unlike him, she had not dared to ask.

Nobody seemed to know any details about Jase's private life. She read the newspapers, of course, with their stories and photographs, gossip about who he was being seen around with. They were always beautiful women, mostly famous, models, actresses—Jase attracted them like eager flies, and it did not take a genius to work out why.

He was a very rich, very successful merchant banker, he was charming, devastatingly attractive with a magnetic sexuality that left most women reeling. What had ever made her think that she had a chance with him?

She pinned a smile on her face and opened the front door. Zack stood outside, smiling.

'Hello,' she said cheerfully, trying to hide her guilt at comparing him to Jase and finding him wanting.

'Hello. You look lovely.' His eyes were openly admiring.

'Thank you. Would you like to come in?'

Zack glanced at his watch. 'We really ought to be going. It's quite a drive and we don't want to miss the beginning of the play.'

'Well, I'm ready,' Lexa smiled, stepping out into the cooler night air.

He was very sweet, she thought, as they drove towards the city, and immediately felt guilty again for the way she was using him.

'Your stepbrother nearly drove me into a ditch as I was turning into your drive,' Zack informed her cheerfully. 'He was certainly in a hurry!'

'Jase?' Lexa questioned lamely, knowing very well that it was.

'Mmm. Came screeching out of the gates like a bat out of hell.' Zack didn't sound at all worried.

'He was probably late,' Lexa replied evenly, though inwardly she felt vaguely worried. It was not like Jase to drive dangerously.

The play was clever, humorous, but Lexa hardly noticed. She sat beside Zack and watched with blank eyes, laughing automatically, clapping automatically.

She was angry with herself for not being able to give it her full attention, but her mind kept shutting out what was happening in front of her, her thoughts veering away, obsessed with Jase, as always.

During the interval she sat in the bar, sipping a glass of chilled white wine, chatting vaguely to Zack. He was an easy undemanding escort, bright and warm, and she found herself liking him more and more as the evening wore on.

After the play, they went to a restaurant that Zack knew well. Lexa found herself actually enjoying her meal, her bleak mood breaking up a little at last.

She asked Zack about his work, fairly safe ground,

she decided, and found it fascinating. He was, primarily, a wild life photographer and had travelled widely, enduring some appalling conditions for good photographs.

'And what about you?' he asked gently. 'Nick tells me you've just got back from Switzerland. Have you got any plans for the future?'

Lexa shrugged her slim shoulders, a sad gesture. 'I wish I had. I've got no idea what I'm going to do. I don't suppose you need an assistant?' she asked jokingly.

'Actually,' Zack was perfectly serious, 'you wouldn't believe it, but I do. Interested?'

'What?' Lexa laughed. 'You're right, I don't believe you.'

Her eyes were very bright, amused, and Zack stared at her, caught still by her beauty.

'No, honestly, I mean it. My present assistant, Mandy, is leaving this month. She's having a baby and she won't be coming back. I was going to advertise, but if you're interested. . . .'

'But I don't know anything about photography!' Lexa protested, admitting to herself that the job did appeal to her, very much.

'It's easy enough to learn,' Zack told her, as though that didn't matter at all. 'So what do you say?'

Lexa did not even need time to think it over. She liked Zack, a lot, and the job sounded fascinating. She had always been interested in photography.

'I say it's a deal—I'd love to work for you,' she said decisively.

'Wonderful! I think this calls for a celebration—just to seal our agreement, you understand. Do you think champagne would be too extravagant?' His boyish face was alight with excitement, pleasure.

'It might be.'

'Surely not.' He ordered it and they toasted their new business relationship. Lexa could hardly believe her good luck. She'd had absolutely no luck at all over the past week looking for a job. Now one had practically fallen into her lap when she was least expecting it.

'When shall I start?' she asked enthusiastically.

'Well, Mandy's leaving on the thirtieth, so you could start on the first of next month, if that suits you.'

'That suits me fine. And thanks, Zack, I appreciate it.' She reached over and gently touched his arm.

'I'm glad to help, and at least it will mean that I see more of you,' he joked, reminding her of the struggle he had had to get her to come out with him tonight. Lexa laughed too, suddenly feeling happy.

Over coffee they talked and talked, not noticing the time flying by. She asked him about himself, and found out that he was thirty years old, unmarried, his parents were Canadian, and he had come to England to attend art college and had stayed on, building up his career.

Looking into his grey eyes, Lexa knew that he was generous, easy-going, even-tempered. He would make a good boss and, more than that, a good friend.

She felt as though she had known him for years, and this was only the second time she had met him. She told him so, and he grimaced.

'I don't know whether I like the sound of that,' he admitted wryly, making her laugh again.

It was very late by the time she got home. She had offered to take a taxi because it seemed unfair that Zack should have to drive her home and then drive all the way back to London, but he wouldn't hear of it, insisting that as he had driven her up to London, it was his prerogative to drive her home again.

'What sort of a man takes a girl out, then leaves her

to make her own way home, because it's more convenient for him?' he asked her, rolling his eyes.

He dropped her at the gates of the house.

'Would you like to come in for some coffee?' she asked, turning to him in the darkness of the car.

He looked at his watch. 'No, I'd better not. It's very late.'

'Thank you for a wonderful evening—and the job.' Lexa leaned over and kissed his cheek.

Zack stared at her. 'We're going to be friends, aren't we?' he said, with wry acceptance.

Lexa smiled, her eyes very gentle. 'I think we are.'

'Pity—I was hoping for more, much more—but then you know that,' he said without reproach.

Lexa bit her lip feeling that she owed him some sort of explanation. 'I'm sorry. There's ... well, there's someone else for me.' She saw his surprise and explained, 'Oh, it's all over now, it's turned completely sour. If I'm honest, it was over before it began, but I can't help the way I feel. You and I—we're just not right for each other, that's why ... why I was so slow to take up your invitation to go out,' she said with slow honesty.

Zack sighed. 'I suppose I knew that tonight, I suppose that's why I offered you the job. At least we know where we stand with each other right from the start.' His voice was dry, regretful.

'Oh, Zack, I am sorry! I didn't mean to ... I wish——'

'Goodnight, Lexa,' he cut in wryly, smiling as he leaned over and flicked open the door for her. 'I'll ring you,' he promised.

'Goodnight, Zack.' Lexa slid out of the car, feeling a warmth around her frozen heart, at his kindness, his understanding.

She walked up the long drive, amazed to find that she was singing to herself.

Jase's car was parked in front of the house. He must be home, she thought happily, forgetting his cruelty for a moment. Then she looked at the watch on her wrist and gasped. It was after one, she and Zack had been talking for *hours*!

She crept quietly into the house, expecting everyone to be in bed, but there was quiet symphony music coming from the drawing room, light issuing from the doorway. Thinking it was Rex and dying to tell somebody her good news, she walked into the room, the smile dying on her lips as her eyes met the frozen golden depths of Jase's.

'Oh! I thought Rex was in here,' she mumbled inanely, stopping in her tracks, glued to the spot and wondering why her legs weren't carrying her quickly away, as she stared at him.

'Rex went to bed hours ago,' Jase drawled softly. He moved gracefully to his feet and she noticed the glass in his hand. 'Would you care for a brandy?'

She hesitated for a moment, surprised by the offer. 'Yes, thank you.' She sat down, curling her feet beneath her, watching him intently as he poured the drinks.

He turned and caught her watching him. Her eyes widened fearfully, pupils dilating, but he smiled gently, taking her breath away.

'Did you enjoy yourself?'

'Yes, it was lovely.' She sipped the brandy slowly, enjoying the warmth sinking unhurriedly down her body, and wondered at his gentleness. Perhaps he did not like to drink alone.

'And the play?' He did not take his eyes off her, yet she could read no expression whatsoever in them.

'I'm afraid I wasn't really paying much attention to it,' she admitted with a small smile.

Jase's dark brows rose. 'You find Zack Harvey that fascinating?' He was teasing her and she laughed.

'No, it wasn't him, it was just that I couldn't concentrate, my mind kept drifting away.'

'I must remember not to go and see it. It doesn't exactly sound riveting,' Jase said drily. He lit a cigarette and Lexa watched him. The lights were low, cocooning them in an atmosphere of warm intimacy. When Jase was in such a gentle mood, her heart ached with love for him.

'I've got some good news,' she said suddenly, wanting to tell him. Really, she wanted to ask about his evening, but her instincts told her that he had been with a woman, and she could not bear to know.

'Tell me.' He slowly exhaled a stream of smoke, his eyes narrowing on her flushed face.

'Zack has offered me a job as his assistant, and I start at the beginning of next month,' she said enthusiastically.

She felt rather than saw Jase stiffen. He was silent.

'Aren't you pleased for me?' she demanded, with a sweet pleading smile.

'Another conquest, Lexa?' The cold words cut through her like a knife, and she frowned.

'No, it's not like that at all. He. . . .' She broke off, jumping to her feet, her eyes filling with painful, unexpected tears. Why should she have to make excuses, give him explanations? Why did she feel so damned guilty when she wasn't? He should be pleased for her, she thought fiercely.

'Why do you have to spoil everything?' she cried miserably, and ran from the room.

CHAPTER SIX

DURING the night there was a violent thunderstorm, the weather finally breaking, and when Lexa woke the next morning, it was raining heavily, the sky dark and overcast.

Tiredly she dragged herself out of bed. As usual, she had not slept well. 'The story of my life,' she muttered to herself, as she dragged her lethargic body into the bathroom to shower.

The storm had brought cooler weather, so she dressed in jeans and an emerald green jumper, then pulled a brush through her hair before going downstairs in search of some coffee.

Luckily, Rex was alone in the dining room. Lexa greeted him, pouring herself some coffee and sipping it gratefully. Her stepfather looked up from his newspaper.

'Good morning, my dear. The weather's broken, it looks like this rain is in for the day.'

'It was getting very close, almost claustrophobic,' said Lexa with feeling.

Rex's eyes sharpened on the empty plate in front of her. 'Won't you have anything to eat?' he asked worriedly. 'Mrs Frone would be glad to prepare anything you want.'

'I'm not very hungry. I hardly ever eat breakfast,' she lied, not wanting any fuss.

Rex frowned, folding his newspaper and placing it on the table, leaning towards her confidentially. 'You're not feeling ill are you, my dear? You're very pale, and frankly, you don't look as though you're sleeping properly. I could ring Bill and ask him to take a look at you, if you're feeling under the weather.' Bill Calder was the local doctor, one of Rex's closest friends, and Lexa shook her head emphatically.

'No, I don't need the doctor. I'm fine, Rex, honestly—a little tired perhaps. Too many late nights, I suppose.' She tried to sound as bright as she possibly could, but even so, she could tell that Rex was not entirely convinced, and cursed herself for not putting on some make-up before she came downstairs.

'Well, if you say so, my dear,' Rex said doubtfully. 'I'm afraid I've been neglecting you since you got back.' And when she shook her head in protest, he added, 'Oh yes, I have. I get so involved with my work, I scarcely have a minute for anything else, but my neglect has been totally unintentional, you must know that. You have settled in all right?'

'Of course I have. I can't remember living anywhere else.' She felt a rush of affection for him, not wanting him to worry about her.

Rex had always been the same. She remembered her mother, mildly grumbling because she could never winkle him out of his study when he was writing.

He was vague and often absentminded, but everyone in the house knew that whenever they needed him, he was there and prepared to drop everything to help them in a crisis.

'It's home,' she repeated, wanting him to know for sure. 'And I'm very happy here.'

'Good, good. I'm glad to hear it.' He seemed satisfied. 'And there's no problem?'

Lexa thought of Jase. 'No problems,' she lied. 'Good news, in fact—I've got a job as Zack Harvey's assistant. He's going to teach me photography, and I start on the first.'

'Is that what you want to do?'

'Yes, I think it is. I'm certainly looking forward to it.' Her voice was bright.

'Well, that is good news. Don't forget to tell Jase that you won't be taking him up on his offer,' Rex reminded her, with a warm smile.

'I've already told him,' she said, swallowing painfully as she remembered his coldness.

'Good, good.' Rex moved slowly to his feet. 'Time to start work. You know where I am if you need me. Don't hesitate to knock on that study door, even if it's only for a chat.'

'I won't,' she promised softly. 'And don't you overwork,' she added sternly.

Her stepfather left the room chuckling, and Lexa poured herself more coffee, staring out at the grey driving rain and wondering what she would do today.

She was glancing idly through Rex's discarded newspaper, reading the review of the play she had seen with Zack, trying to work out why her memory of it didn't tally with anything the newspaper critic said, when Marny wandered into the dining room on bare feet, her slender model's body wrapped in a blue Japanese kimono, her hand over her mouth as she yawned.

'I thought you were at work,' said Lexa, pushing aside the newspaper, glad of some company.

'Day off,' Marny replied groggily, pushing back her cloud of tousled dark hair. 'Any coffee left?'

Lexa lifted the lid of the pot. 'Only a drop. I'll go and make some more, I could do with another cup myself,' she said cheerfully as she got to her feet.

When she returned with the fresh coffee, Marny was peeling an orange, looking more awake, glaring out of the window at the rain, as Lexa had been doing only fifteen minutes before. The older girl gratefully sipped the coffee Lexa poured for her, and smiled. 'Ah, that's better! My mind won't work until I've had my morning cup of coffee.'

Lexa told her about her new job and was congratulated.

'I knew Zack Harvey wasn't going to give up easily,' said Marny, with a knowing look on her face.

'It's strictly business. We're just friends,' Lexa said firmly.

'That's what they all say.' Marny finished her orange, delicately wiping her fingers. 'Mind you, he is rather handsome.'

Lexa ignored that. 'What are you going to do today? Anything special?'

Marny grimaced at the weather. 'I was intending to laze about in the sun doing absolutely nothing. So much for that——' Her voice stopped abruptly.

Lexa had her back to the door, but she knew, as Marny's eyes widened and a faint flush touched her cheekbones, that Jase had just entered the room.

She watched from the corner of her eye as he poured himself some coffee and sat down, leaning back with relaxed indolence, as he surveyed the two girls.

'You're up late,' Marny teased him.

'On the contrary, my child, I've been up for hours,' he replied with a lazy smile.

Lexa concentrated on the folded newspaper in front of her, pretending some desperate interest in the tiny black print.

'I've got an idea,' she heard Marny saying excitedly. 'Jase darling, why don't you take Lexa and me out for lunch? We could drive to the country and stop at one of those tiny little pubs. Do say yes!' Lexa's heart sank as she listened to Marny's proposition. She had absolutely no intention of spending the day with Jase. Marny was welcome to him!

She glanced up at the older girl. Marny was staring at Jase, waiting for his answer, her eyes bright and beautiful and beseeching, she shifted her glance to Jase and found that he was watching her, his eyes guarded. She flushed and lowered her head.

'It's not exactly the weather for driving in the country,' she heard him finally reply in a low drawling voice.

'That wouldn't matter,' Marny persisted cheerfully. 'We could still enjoy ourselves.'

'Sorry, Marny, I don't have the time today,' he said firmly, gently, and Lexa knew that he was looking at her again, so she kept her head down.

'You could make the time,' Marny sounded sullen.

Jase got to his feet, stretching his arms above his head, drawing both girl's eyes to the power of his body.

'Don't sulk,' he told Marny, with a faintly indulgent smile.

But Marny was not going to give in. 'Jase, couldn't . . .?'

'I've told you, I'm too damned busy. So let's just drop the subject shall we?' Suddenly there was a rough irritated edge to his voice, and daring to glance up at him for a second, Lexa saw the lines of strain around his mouth, the impatience in his hooded golden eyes.

Marny got to her feet, and only Lexa could see the brightness of unshed tears in her eyes.

'You swine,' she said lightly, too lightly, and without looking at either Lexa or Jase, walked from the room with her head held high.

Lexa heard Jase sigh, and glared at him. 'Why were you so unkind?' she demanded, hating him for being so brutal. She knew what Marny was going through, and her heart contracted with compassion, Jase had treated her in much the same way. Marny was probably sobbing her heart out now. Lexa's sympathy rose. She had been there, she knew the agony of caring too much for Jase.

'Why the hell do you think?' he replied flatly.

'You could have let her down lightly,' Lexa said stubbornly, refusing to be intimidated.

'And you're an expert on that, aren't you?' came the cold, cutting reply.

'You could have, it wouldn't have hurt you,' she insisted.

His eyes flashed fire at her and she could feel her heart beating very fast.

'It would have hurt her,' he said roughly. 'Do you think she wanted to cry in front of you, in front of me? She has her pride, and I didn't want to grind it in the dust, despite what you think.'

Lexa stared at him in surprise. 'I don't understand. . . .' she began, a frown pleating her smooth forehead.

'Forget it,' Jase advised coolly, walking over to the windows and staring out over the wet gardens. Lexa's eyes were hungrily drawn to the tense powerful line of his shoulders beneath the thin shirt he wore. Had she misjudged him?

'Tell me,' she begged quietly. 'Please, Jase, I'd like to understand. Are you really too busy?'

'Yes, I'm really too busy.' His voice was expressionless.

'You know Marny's in love with you, don't you?' Light had dawned and she realised what Jase had been doing. She *had* misjudged him.

'Of course she's not in love with me,' he stated calmly. 'Infatuated maybe, but that will pass.' He paused, placing a cigarette between his lips and lighting it before continuing. 'As long as I don't encourage her, and taking her out for lunch is my idea of encouragement.'

Lexa stared at the long hard sweep of his back. 'I still don't understand why you couldn't be nicer to her.'

Jase swore under his breath. 'Dammit, Lexa, use your brain! I'm not responsible for the way she feels, but I don't want to hurt her deliberately,' he snapped with exaggerated patience. 'And it would hurt her if she thought I pitied her. She was prepared to push the issue of lunch, so I had to slap her down hard. I didn't enjoy it, but perhaps now she'll realise I'm not some sort of knight in shining armour.'

'I'm sorry, I do understand now. I misjudged you,' Lexa admitted quietly.

Jase turned slowly, staring at her. 'That's quite an admission coming from you,' he said with a slight smile. Lexa shrugged, feeling her face running high with colour, her mouth going dry at the charm in his smile. She still felt guilty at the way she had misunderstood his actions concerning Marny.

As far as Jase was concerned, Marny was his sister. He was perceptive enough to be aware of her infatuation but sensitive and caring enough not to take advantage of the situation. He was trying to do the best thing for her, not encouraging her, showing her that he was human, not the idol she had built him up into.

Did he also know that Lexa was in love with him? She turned away from that thought fearfully, certain that he did not love her.

She suddenly felt trapped. The house was full of tensions. She supposed it was inevitable, the family was so diverse. They weren't a real family at all. Rex held them all together, and yet he was totally unaware of the present undercurrents. It was ironic that they were all trying to protect him, and in doing so were themselves falling apart.

As though reading her mind, Jase suddenly said, extremely casually, 'I'm flying back to the States the day after tomorrow.'

The news hit Lexa like a blow to the stomach. She couldn't bear him to go. It was the moment she had been dreading, inevitable, terrible. She looked at him, deathly pale, her green eyes shadowed. 'Why?' she asked huskily.

'Business calls me. I've been lazing round here far too long,' he said with a smile.

'You've been working in London and Birmingham,' she protested, staring at him as though at any moment she expected him to disappear into thin air. She had a sickening feeling that she would never see him again. Crazy, said her head, but her heart was crying.

'My real work is in New York,' Jase told her lazily.

He was so calm. How could he be so calm, so uncaring? He was going away and she desperately needed him to stay.

'Don't go.' The words were whispered before she realised they had left her mouth. 'If Nick could hear you now,' Jase mocked coolly.

'I don't care about Nick!' she cried desperately. 'Don't go, Jase.'

He moved towards her slowly, his face suddenly very gentle. He touched her hair. 'I have to,' he murmured, staring into her face as though trying to memorise every soft line of it.

'When will you come back?' She wanted a date, a time to the minute when she would see him again. She couldn't let him go, without knowing when he would come back. Let him go? The words echoed hollowly around her shocked brain. He did not belong to her. But I love him, she thought fiercely, that should give me some rights.

'I don't know.' There was a shadowed anguish in his eyes, his long fingers straying from her hair to her face, stroking over the soft skin. He smiled. 'And if you're honest, you'll have to admit that things will be a lot easier round here when I'm gone, especially for Marny and Nick.'

'But not for me!' She couldn't stop the tears that were all at once falling down her cheeks.

'Even for you, Lexa,' Jase said gently. He looked into her haunted face and a second later pulled her into his arms, holding her tightly, convulsively. She pressed herself close to the hard warmth of his body, sure that she would die if he left her. She could feel the immense strength of the arms that held her, the steady rise and fall of his chest beneath her cheek, and desire began to tingle deep in her stomach.

Acting on an impulse she could not control, made desperate by the fact that her time with him was short, she lifted her head, reaching up to frame his lean face with her hands, putting her mouth to his and kissing him.

She felt the stillness in him for a second, but he could not resist her, and his mouth hungrily parted hers, his arms tightening around her almost immediately.

He kissed her with deep possession and she could feel the racing of his heart against her body, matching her own quickening heart, beat for beat.

She could not think, knowing only the hungry pleasure of his mouth. Her small hands tangled in the thickness of his hair and she moaned softly as his lips slid to her throat, his fingers sliding beneath her emerald jumper to find the warm softness of her body.

He was breathing raggedly, her skin was warm satin beneath his seeking fingers, he could barely contain his need for her and it took all his control to lift his mouth from her vulnerable throat, after long sweet moments.

They stared into each other's eyes. Lexa could see the desire burning in the golden depths, tenderness, hunger, and she pressed herself even closer to the hard length of him.

'I love you, Jase,' she whispered softly, her eyes dark with that love, as she looked into his face.

His body stiffened against hers and he expelled his breath very slowly.

'Lexa, you don't know what you're saying,' he muttered thickly. His eyes were suddenly shuttered, blank, closing away his thoughts, his feelings.

'Yes, I do,' she said, the soft smile fading slowly from her mouth. She was realising what she had said, what she had given away in those desire-filled seconds when she had wanted him to know the truth, his words hitting her like a shower of freezing cold water. It had been a moment of utter madness, and she would probably have to pay for it now.

'What the hell do you know about love, about men?' Jase demanded harshly. 'Lexa you're too young— you're a baby, only just finished with school. You have the world at your feet!'

'I'm twenty years old, Jase, not a child, so don't treat me like one.' She pulled herself away from him in despair, feeling terribly embarrassed. Whatever had possessed her to reveal her most precious secret to him? He did not want her love, he was making that crystal clear.

Jase raked a hand through his black hair, swearing savagely. 'I'm sorry, that was bloody clumsy, I didn't mean—hell, Lexa, you know what I'm trying to say to you.' His words were tense, low.

'Do I?' She stared at him, masking her hurt with scornful pride.

'Your life is just beginning, you still have to learn about love, you're blinded by films and books and adolescent dreams, life is not like that. You don't love me, I only wish——' He stopped abruptly, biting off the terse rapid words.

Lexa stared at him, feeling as though her heart was breaking. He only wished that she had not mentioned it, had not embarrassed them both.

'No, perhaps you're right perhaps I don't love you,' she said in a cold clear voice that she hardly recognised as her own.

She wanted to hurt him as he had hurt her, a blind painful desire for revenge. She had offered him love, and she *did* love him with all her heart. He had thrown it back in her face. As far as he was concerned, she was just an adolescent dreamer.

He saw her as he saw Marny, an irritation to be indulged, yet neatly side-stepped.

Jase's mouth twisted in a humourless smile. 'I'm glad to hear it,' he said coolly.

She could have sworn she saw tenderness glimmering in the depths of his eyes as he added, 'Don't tempt me with your schoolgirl fairytales, Lexa—I might be tempted to do something we'd both regret.'

'Why stop now? Regret seems to play a large part in your life,' she retorted coldly. 'Tell me, do you have any regrets about Eva?'

She saw a faint flicker in his eyes, his mouth hard with cynical amusement. 'I thought Nick wouldn't be able to keep his mouth shut,' he drawled softly.

'Nick told me all about it. Why shouldn't he?' Lexa

demanded belligerently.

'Why indeed? Your relationship is, shall we say, intimate. So what do you know about Eva?' He was calm, totally in control, there was not the merest hint of expression in his face or his voice.

'I know that you stole her from Nick, made her pregnant and then abandoned her,' she said succinctly, feeling a sharp spark of triumph at the tightening of his jaw.

'And knowing all this, not forgetting the fact that you're sleeping with my brother, how can you imagine yourself in love with me?' Jase asked smoothly, placing faint emphasis on the word 'imagine'.

Lexa closed her eyes. He had not denied any of it, not a single word. Had she expected him to? Yes, she had. She had been clinging to the vain belief that Nick had somehow got it wrong, that there must be some reasonable explanation. How stupid she was, stupid stupid, *stupid*!

Nick had been right all along. She looked at Jase's hard-boned face and her heart twisted.

Even if. . . . Her mind halted. Even though Nick's story about Eva was true, she still loved Jase. She would have forgiven him anything. Not that it made any difference. He did not love her. She said the words over to herself; they hurt like nothing else could.

'How can you be so cruel?' she asked confusedly.

'How can you be so bloody stupid?' he countered savagely, lighting another cigarette with violent hands, echoing her own opinion of herself at that moment.

'I don't know.' She lifted her hands in despair, aware of the fierce shocking tension in him. Her stupidity was as much of a mystery to her as it apparently was to him.

She had been a fool to think that she could come

back here. The Fallons were a dangerous breed, and it was time to get away. Lexa felt unbearably confused, unbearably hurt. Jase's rejection of her had not yet fully sunk in, she was too busy fighting with him, trying to regain her battered pride.

She had the compelling urge to run from the room, but to do that was to admit defeat. She was not going to run away even though she knew she was wasting her time. She would never be able to pierce Jase's skin. He would always win in any battles they had. He was cold and hard and far too clever.

She thought about herself and Marny and the unknown Eva. They all wanted Jase; they had all lost him.

'I'm glad you're going back to New York,' she said childishly.

'Not half as glad as I am, believe me.' There was an edge of utter weariness in his words, to which her heart reacted, but her head ignored. It seemed to her to be a final rejection.

'I hope I never see you again,' she added vehemently for good measure. There was nothing else to say, so she turned on her heel and slowly left the room.

She wanted to look back, to see him just once more, but she forced herself not to. What was the point? His image was burned on her memory, her heart, and if she turned back, she would probably do something humiliating like running into his arms.

She walked upstairs unhurriedly. Her legs felt heavy, very tired. Her vision was blurred. She dashed away the tears from her face with angry fingers. She did not want to cry.

As she reached the landing, she briefly wondered where Marny was, but turned towards her own room.

She could not offer Marny any comfort. She could not even comfort herself.

As she lay on her bed with her tears pouring uncontrollably down her face, she wondered how she could have made such a fool of herself. Jase had warned her right from the beginning, but she had blundered on, not believing his cold cruelty, not believing Nick.

Well, she was paying for her stupidity now. She had forced Jase into a situation where he had had to lay the facts on the line, had to tell her that he did not want her love. She had brought this agony on herself, and in two days Jase was leaving. She might not ever see him again.

She turned her face into the pillow and let her tears carry her into the dark oblivion of sleep.

CHAPTER SEVEN

EXACTLY a year later, almost to the day, Lexa hurried through the passenger lounge at Heathrow Airport, as her flight was called.

Zack was waiting for her at the gate, his face calm, smiling. She hurried towards him, hoisting her heavy bag higher on her shoulder.

'I thought you weren't going to make it,' he greeted her casually, pulling the bag from her shoulder and swinging it on to his own.

'I always make it,' Lexa told him with a smile, as they walked through, towards the plane.

Time had been tight, though. She had been caught in a traffic jam caused by an accident and had had to rush like mad to get to the airport. As she fastened herself into her seat, her mind slid back to another plane, a year ago, when she had been coming back from Switzerland. It seemed years and years ago. So much had happened since she sat on that plane, she could hardly recognise herself as she had been a year ago— gauche, naïve, stupidly innocent. She felt nothing but self-contempt for the way she had acted then.

'Penny for them.' Zack's voice cut into her thoughts from beside her.

Lexa shrugged her slim shoulders, wishing that the 'no smoking' light would flash off so that she could have a cigarette. 'I was thinking of the last time I was on a plane, when I came back from Switzerland.' She kept her voice deliberately vague, not really wanting to talk, and settled back in her seat and closed her eyes.

She was looking forward to this holiday. She needed it. Time to relax and take things easy, to forget all the tensions of day-to-day living. Although she had to admit that working for Zack had certainly taken her mind off her problems, he moved at such a breathtaking pace that she frequently found herself exhausted, open-mouthed at his boundless energy.

She felt herself drifting into a light half-sleep. She had been up until after two that morning at a party. Not very wise, she supposed, in view of this early flight, but she had felt like dancing, surrounding herself with people.

The next thing she was aware of was Zack lightly shaking her arm. 'Wake up, Lexa! We've arrived.'

Her eyes snapped open. It couldn't be true! She had only closed her eyes a couple of minutes ago. She stared out of the tiny plastic window and saw the Nice Airport building, the sun blinding on the runway.

She turned to Zack with wide eyes. 'Why did you . . .?'

'You looked like you needed the rest,' he told her cheerfully.

Lexa raised her eyebrows and pulled a mirror and brush out of her handbag. 'Thanks, Zack,' she said with dry sweetness, making him laugh.

She coaxed her blonde curls into some sort of order, grimacing at her reflection before snapping shut the mirror. Then she got to her feet, smoothing down the fine cotton of her blouse, her tight jeans, and they left the plane.

There were two hired cars waiting for them, one for Lexa to drive to Rex's villa and one for Zack to drive to his business appointment in Antibes.

Unlike Lexa, Zack was in France on business and it had been his idea that they fly down together. He enjoyed her company.

Lexa slung her suitcase into the back of the little white car and stuck her sunglasses on her nose, revelling in the bright relentless sunlight. She intended to get a good tan while she was here.

'So what's the plan?' she asked Zack, as she slid into the car.

'Well, I hope, I'll be back for dinner,' he said, dropping a kiss on her soft blonde hair. She had given him a map by which to find the villa.

'I'll buy some food,' she said thoughtfully, planning her day. 'Unless you want to eat out?'

'Your cooking is fine by me.' He looked at his watch. 'I'll have to dash. See you tonight.'

She watched him shoot away and smiled. She wasn't in a particularly energetic mood and eating in tonight would suit her fine.

She bought steak and salad and fruit, crisp French bread and a number of other things she thought of at the last minute, then manoeuvred the car out of Nice and up the narrow, twisting road to the villa. It was not far, which was a relief, as she felt very thirsty. I should have had a drink in Nice, she thought to herself as the car climbed higher.

At last the villa came in sight, low and white, overlooking the startlingly blue Mediterranean. She parked the car and carried the food in first, knowing a moment of panic when she could not find the keys. She found them, not in her handbag, where she expected them to be, but in the pocket of her jacket. She sighed with relief. She could so easily have forgotten them altogether, the state she had been in that morning.

The interior was cool and dim. She walked through

the marble-floored hallway, throwing open all the doors, enjoying the peaceful solitude. She hadn't been here since the year her mother married Rex. The three of them and Marny had spent a month of the summer here. It hadn't changed at all.

She walked into the lounge and pushed open the long windows and the slatted wooden blinds. Sunlight poured in and she wandered on to the terrace, gazing at the glittering swimming pool, the rattan furniture, the profusion of flowers and olive trees in the garden. Below, the sea sparkled, dotted with boats, and she could see the modern white hotel blocks of Nice, serene in the sunshine. It was beautiful, the perfect place for a holiday.

In the kitchen she switched on the refrigerator and stored away the food. She had no idea when the villa had last been used, but there was plenty of dried and tinned food, coffee and biscuits.

She ground some coffee and switched on the ancient-looking percolator, then went to fetch her case.

There were four bedrooms and she chose one at random, flinging her case on the bed and leaving it. Her sandals clattered noisily on the tiled floors and she kicked them off, enjoying the icy coolness beneath her bare feet.

She drank two cups of coffee and ate a peach, sitting on the terrace, staring out at the view, lifting her face to the sun. Then she took a cool shower and slept the afternoon away.

She woke at six feeling refreshed and alert and dressed in white trousers and a pale green silk blouse, amazed that she had slept so long. She obviously needed a holiday more than she had realised.

The air was a little cooler now. She wandered into the lounge, staring round at the shelves full of books, the framed charcoal drawings on the pale walls, the comfortable furniture. Rex had won this villa on a wager, the story went, and Lexa could well believe it.

She had heard the wild tales about him; one only had to look in his eyes to see the wisdom, the experience and even now, a certain wildness. She sank into one of the chairs. Rex had been pleased that she was taking a holiday. She had visited him only a few days before, to ask permission to use the villa.

It seemed such a long time since she had lived at the house. She had moved out just after Jase had returned to the States.

Jase. Whatever she was thinking about, whatever she was doing, he was constantly in her thoughts. She had not seen him for a year, she had not seen him since she had blurted out her love for him and he had rejected her.

She had deliberately gone up to London the day he left, so that she would not have to see him again. She could not have faced him, she doubted that she could face him even now, and a year had passed.

After he left, a kind of strained normality had settled on the house. For Lexa, it had been difficult to live there, for her, the house had been full of memories of Jase. So when she had started working for Zack, she had realised that she had a perfect excuse for moving out.

Luckily, one of Marny's modelling friends had vacated her flat in Kensington, and Lexa had snapped it up, moving in within the month. She had dreaded telling Rex, and looking back at that dread, she realised how silly it had been. Rex had been utterly delighted for her, glad that she was spreading her wings and becoming independent. Marny, waiting to see what Rex's reaction would be, had confided that she too was thinking of moving out. Up to now, however, she had done nothing about it, and Lexa wondered if she ever would, because despite what she sometimes said, Marny loved living in the big old house with Rex. For her, it was well worth the inconvenience of a long journey up to London every day. And unlike Lexa, Marny seemed to have got over her desire for Jase. At the moment, she was heavily involved with a record producer. They had been seeing each other for nine months and it seemed serious, although Lexa did not know for sure.

Sometimes, she thought that Marny was trying too desperately to wipe Jase from her heart. There was often a fever about the older girl that was vaguely frightening, all the more frightening because Lexa knew exactly what Marny had been through, could match the feelings in herself.

Lexa was involved with nobody. Her heart was filled with Jase, even though he was thousands of miles away and she had not seen him for ages. She was cool and friendly with men she met, but could not help comparing these men to Jase. They never matched up. How long would it take, she asked herself despairingly, how long before she could look at somebody and *not* compare them to Jase?

Feeling the beginnings of a grey depression drifting into her brain, she poured herself a Martini, filling her glass with ice cubes, then she wandered out on to the the terrace, breathing in the perfumed air.

She had changed in the last twelve months. She had grown up. Now, she was cool and sophisticated, mature, and she had a carefully built wall around her heart that nobody got through.

It still made her cringe inwardly, though, when she thought about her behaviour with Jase. She had flung herself at him, desperately hurt when he rejected her so brutally, although now she could see that he had no choice. She could not blame him, which was a pity, she thought wryly, because it only strengthened her love and respect for him.

If he had treated her badly, with total disregard, she could have used that to try and kill her love for him. As it was, she had only his kindness, his gentleness, and passion to remember him by. It only made her long for him more.

She heard the roar of a car engine on the still air, pulling alongside the villa and cutting out. Zack was here.

Lexa ran through the hall and opened the door, smiling at him as he climbed out of the car. 'You're early.'

'I got it all sorted out pretty quickly.' He kissed her cheek, grey eyes assessing. 'You look good.'

'I've been asleep all afternoon, so I feel full of energy.'

'Lucky you!'

They went inside and Lexa showed him to his room.

'This is great,' he remarked, opening the windows and looking out at the view.

He was only staying for one night, then driving on to Cannes to do some filming on the coast. Lexa was staying on at the villa, not accompanying him, and if he finished his work early, he would probably spend a few more days at the villa before they returned to England.

'I'll start dinner,' Lexa said brightly, and left the room, her depression vanishing.

In the kitchen she put the steaks on to grill and prepared a salad, singing to herself.

Ten minutes later Zack appeared beside her, his fair hair dark with water from the shower, a bottle of wine in his hand.

'Can I help?'

'You could open that wine,' she said, carefully blending the salad dressing with a fork, adding a little more black pepper.

They ate on the terrace, both in a holiday mood. The sea was hazy and Lexa slowly sipped her wine, watching Zack as he ate.

They had become very close friends over the past twelve months, and were very fond of each other.

'Mmm, wonderful!' Zack pushed away his plate and sat back with a replete sigh. 'You certainly know how to cook!'

She laughed. 'Grilling two steaks is hardly cooking!'

'So you say—I wouldn't know. Burning a piece of toast is difficult for me.'

Lexa pulled a face at him. That was true enough. Zack always ate out or ordered food to be sent in.

'What you need is a good woman,' she told him teasingly, half seriously. Zack's relationships with women always seemed to end in disaster, and it wasn't because the ladies involved were not keen. Lexa couldn't understand it.

'So why don't you take pity on me and marry me?' he suggested lightly, though his eyes shifted away from hers.

'You haven't asked me,' Lexa parried, laughingly, imagining him to be joking.

'Believe me, I would if I thought there was the slightest chance that you'd accept.' He was suddenly deadly serious, and the atmosphere changed in an instant, becoming tense, ominous.

Lexa stiffened, hearing the low drawl underlying his words. That transatlantic drawl always appeared strongly when he was tense or angry, giving him away.

She stared at him with wide, slightly fearful eyes.

'What ... what are you saying?' she asked worriedly, knowing that she should have laughed, said something cool and witty to lighten the atmosphere and cover up her apprehension. Zack was silent for a moment, then he smiled, his grey eyes warm and friendly again.

'Don't panic, Lexa. Forget I said anything, okay?'

She frowned, thinking how impossible that would be. 'Okay.' She wished she didn't sound so halfhearted She lit a cigarette, aware that he was watching her, her mind racing.

There had never been anything but affectionate friendship between them, it had been an unspoken rule made that first night they went to the theatre together. Were Zack's feelings stronger than she knew? She had been too caught up with her own bruised heart, too self-obsessed to have noticed anything developing. She glanced up at him, feeling apprehensive, to find him still gazing at her, his expression curious.

'Have I worried you?' he asked gently.

She was too confused to be anything other than honest. 'A little.'

'I'm sorry.' His shoulders hunched in a kind of defeat and Lexa sighed touching his arm.

'I'm sorry too. I ... well, I. ...' She broke off, unable to find the right words.

'Is it still that other man?' Zack asked quietly, watching the sudden flush that crept up her cheeks, the haunted sadness that shadowed her eyes. They gave him his answer more surely than words.

'He must have hurt you pretty badly.'

Lexa was silent. Yes, Jase had hurt her, but not by anything he'd done. He could not help it, could not be blamed because he did not love her.

'You ought to talk about it,' Zack persisted gently.

'I've watched you bottling it up for more than a year now, and it can't be doing you any good.'

'I've never talked about it to anybody,' she admitted wryly, prepared to believe that he was right.

'I'll always be around if you want to,' Zack smiled, sensing that she couldn't be pushed. 'You know, you've changed a lot since I first met you.'

'For the better, I hope,' she said, trying to sound light.

'You're different.' His voice was thoughtful. 'It's difficult to put my finger on it. You seem to be surrounded by a shell of ice, you're cool and untouchable, you rarely show your feelings to the world. What happened, Lexa, to freeze you like this?'

He was trying to help, she knew that, but what could she say? He had never mentioned it before. It was probably the warm, intimate atmosphere, the fact that they were not working tonight as they usually were when they dined together.

'You must be imagining it,' she said cheerfully, carefully. 'I'm just the same as I always was.' But Zack shook his head, undeflected.

'It isn't just me, Nick has noticed it as well.'

Lexa smiled, thinking of her stepbrother.

'I haven't seen Nick for ages. I could have had a head transplant and he wouldn't know!'

Nick was touring America with his jazz band. The last time Lexa had seen him, had been at Christmas. They were friends again now, but not as close. That summer had affected them all, and Nick's lies to Jase had somehow severed some of the bonds of affection between them. Lexa did not blame him any more, and her anger and bitterness were long gone, but the damage had been done and ther had been no way to repair it—they had both recognised that with great sadness.

'And he's terrible at letters. I think I've only had three postcards since he left. Have you heard from him?'

'One—no, two postcards,' Zack said laughingly. 'And you're changing the subject, my darling.'

'Yes, I suppose I am. If you really want to know, I fell in love with somebody who didn't love me. That's all there is to it.' Her voice was flat and uninformative.

'He must have been crazy,' Zack said huskily.

Lexa laughed harshly. 'I'd like to think so, but I know it's not true. The worst thing was that I made a terrible fool of myself—something I don't like to remember.'

'And you don't intend to do that again in a hurry,' said Zack with sudden understanding. 'Hence the wall of ice.'

'I don't intend to do it again, full stop,' she replied firmly, vehemently, inhaling deeply on her cigarette, her hands trembling.

It was the first time she had ever mentioned what had happened to anybody, and it was quite terrifying, although she knew Zack was right, it was doing her good to talk about it. It had been walled up inside her for so long. Too long.

'You don't cut down the apple tree because you find one rotten apple growing on it,' Zack said softly.

'You do if the rotten apple is bigger than the tree,' she retorted sadly. 'Oh, I know what you're thinking, that I've allowed it to get completely out of proportion. Obviously I don't think I have. It was the first time I'd fallen in love and I was young and inexperienced and so *stupid*, I can hardly bear to think about it, but I haven't got over it, Zack, I still love him, I think I always will, and that's so frightening that if I ever do get over him, I certainly don't intend to make the same mistake again—not ever!' She angrily brushed away the rush of tears that were blurring her vision. 'So now you know,' she finished with a weak, shaky smile.

Zack's face was very serious, his eyes compassionate. 'I'm sorry, I didn't mean to pry or upset you.'

'You were only trying to help.' She could not bear him to feel bad about it. 'And you were right, I think it is better to talk about it than to bottle it all up.'

'My reasons were purely selfish,' he admitted heavily. 'I wanted to know the situation because I ... well, because I care for you a hell of a lot.' He smiled wryly. 'I hoped that maybe there was a chance for me.'

'Oh, Zack!' She felt the tears filling her eyes again. 'You're so sweet.'

'Sweet?' His mouth twisted self-deprecatingly. 'That sounds suspiciously like an insult!'

But his eyes were laughing as he got to his feet. 'I'll wash up, seeing you did the cooking. Do you fancy hitting the high spots of Nice tonight?'

Their easy friendship was back on its old footing again and Zack was trying hard to regain their usual rapport, perhaps a little embarrassed by his persistent questioning.

'Yes, it sounds like fun,' Lexa agreed, her smile telling him that he had not offended her. 'And as you're in such a generous mood, you can make the coffee.'

An hour and a half later, they left the villa and drove into Nice in Zack's car.

Lexa had changed into a sleeveless emerald green dress, with a tight bodice and a full skirt that flared softly around her slim legs. She looked good, and Zack's long whistle when he saw her proved it and bolstered her confidence.

The night was warm, balmy, the stars huge and twinkling in the soft darkness of the sky. The sun roof was open on the car and Lexa could feel the breeze blowing through her hair as the car shot down towards Nice.

It was crowded, busy, full of light and life. They parked and wandered round hand in hand before Zack led her to an expensive club on the Promenade des Anglais.

Inside, the lights were dim, the music for dancing. They sat down and ordered drinks, and before Lexa had time to catch her breath, they were suddenly surrounded by people, crowding round their table. Zack was making introductions, introducing her to Clea and Larry, both tall and fair, Bess and Jean-Paul, Jean-Paul with dark, smouldering French looks and Bess, small and black-haired, reminding Lexa of Marny, and a tall tanned man on his own, called Bruce, who was eyeing Lexa with undisguised admiration and interest.

'I arranged it, I'm afraid,' Zack murmured against her ear. 'I thought it would be good for us tonight.' Lexa kissed him, grateful for his understanding.

More drinks were ordered and everybody was talking at once. Jean-Paul and Bruce were going to be working with Zack in Cannes, and Clea and Larry were old friends who had been living in Nice for years.

Lexa found herself relaxing, enjoying herself. She danced until her feet ached with Zack and Bruce and chatted to Bess. They seemed to get on right away, something sparking between them, both giggling at the same jokes, kindred spirits.

The evening sped by like a flash of light and all too soon it was time to go back to the villa. Bess and Jean-Paul were staying with Clea and Larry and Lexa arranged to have lunch there the following day, smiling happily as they invited her.

It was so nice to find friends here, because she would

be on her own when Zack left for Cannes. She could feel her eyelids drooping as they climbed the mountain road and as soon as they reached the villa, she clambered out of the car, dropping with tiredness.

'No stamina, that's your trouble,' Zack told her, sliding an arm round her shoulders and leading her inside.

'I've been working for you for a year—that's what I call stamina!' she retorted with an exhausted smile.

He tilted up her face with his fingers and stared thoughtfully down at her. 'Goodnight, Lexa.' He bent his head and briefly touched her mouth with his.

The kiss was pleasant, undemanding, and Lexa kissed him back before turning away. 'Goodnight,' she said softly, and slipped inside her bedroom.

She slept well that night, waking from a deep dreamless sleep after eight the next morning. She took a shower, turning the taps on to cold, gasping beneath the jets of freezing water, washing until her body tingled all over, then tied her hair back and dressed in a sleeveless blue sundress with an embroidered yoke, before leaving her room in search of breakfast, feeling ravenously hungry.

Zack was on the terrace, reading a French newspaper and drinking coffee. He looked up as Lexa approached, his smile bright. 'Up at last!' he teased, grey eyes twinkling.

'Where did you get that?' she pointed to the newspaper.

'Same place I got those.' He indicated a plate of fresh warm croissants on the table in front of him. 'I drove into Nice. I knew you wouldn't be up for hours.'

'How lovely!' She sat down and poured herself some coffee. 'Fresh croissants—now I really know I'm in France!' She reached for one and cut into it, spreading it with golden butter that melted as it touched the warm bread, and rich cherry conserve. 'I suppose I'd better make the most of these.' She wrinkled her nose at him. 'Once you've gone to Cannes, there'll be nobody to bring me croissants in the morning.'

Zack laughed at her mournful face. 'I'm sure Bruce would be more than happy to oblige if he wasn't coming to Cannes with me. Come to think of it, I'm damned glad that he is!'

Lexa laughed too, yet she knew that beneath the light tone, Zack was serious. And that worried her. She gazed out over the garden and ate her breakfast in silence, breathing deeply, the morning air perfumed and warm, promising fierce heat later on.

'What time will you be leaving?' She glanced at Zack to find him watching her.

'After breakfast.' He looked at his watch. 'I'm picking up Bruce and Jean-Paul at ten. Will you be okay on your own for a few days?' He sounded worried.

'I came here for peace and quiet,' Lexa reminded him. 'I'm going to do absolutely nothing and enjoy every minute of it.'

'I'll ring you tomorrow,' he promised, and Lexa agreed.

He did worry so. She watched him as he returned his attention to the newspaper. French was his second language; having been brought up in Canada, he could read it easily.

She was so fond of him. She let her eyes wander over his long fair hair, the sharp lines of his face, his lean muscular body. She had the feeling that he was half way to being in love with her, and that was worrying because she did not want to hurt him.

She was as blind as a bat sometimes, she thought miserably. How could she have let things get to this state without even noticing? The first hint she'd had was yesterday when Zack had asked her about Jase.

Inwardly sighing, she finished her coffee then wandered into the wild garden, bending her head to the roses and geraniums, inhaling their sweet scents. My life shouldn't be so messy, she thought ruefully. Everybody else seems to handle things fine. Why not me?

Zack kissed her fiercely as he left. 'Take care of yourself,' he told her firmly. 'You've got my number.'

'Don't fuss,' she replied lightly, waving as the car pulled away, towards the road.

She washed the breakfast dishes then lay in the sun, letting her mind drift, until it was time to drive into Nice for lunch with Bess and Clea.

She found the house easily, in one of the larger back streets. It was tall and thin and painted a dark pink, with tiny balconies and white wooden blinds on the upstairs windows. The front door was open, but Lexa rang the bell anyway. Bess came to the door, her dark hair in plaits wrapped around her head, wearing tight red shorts and a red tee-shirt.

Her smile was friendly, welcoming. 'Come in! I'm so glad you came. We're all up on the roof.'

She led the way through the dim hall, up what seemed to Lexa like endless flights of stairs, finally emerging into the sunlight and a tiny rooftop garden, where Clea and another woman lay reclining on sunloungers, chatting.

'You know Clea, of course, and this is Eva Sutherland, Clea's best friend. Eva—Lexa Matthews.'

Eva smiled. 'Hello, Lexa, nice to meet you.'

She was young and very pretty, Lexa thought as she returned the greeting, with short auburn hair wisping around her finely-boned face.

Bess was rushing about. 'Would you like a cold

drink? This is Clea's own recipe, full of tropical fruit.' Lexa sat down, nodding.

'Eva arrived this morning,' Bess told her. 'She works in Monte Carlo, but she's on holiday for a few weeks.'

Everyone chatted until lunch. It was all very friendly and Lexa enjoyed herself immensely. They were vibrant, intelligent women, good company. She learned that Bess and Jean-Paul lived in Paris; only married for two years, they seemed very happy. Clea and Larry had moved to Nice, so that Larry could paint.

They had all known Zack for years, and they all wondered if Lexa was his girl-friend. She explained the situation, explained about her job and explained that she was on holiday.

Over a lunch of salad and cold meat, so many varieties that Lexa was wide-eyed, followed by fresh fruit, Bess suggested that they did some sightseeing together.

'We could go to the old town and the museums—and how about Grasse? Oh yes, and we could visit Vence, it's only about fifteen miles away. What do you think?'

'Suits me,' Lexa agreed. 'It's not much fun sightseeing on your own.' Clea and Eva declined the offer. Clea had seen all the sights and Eva wanted to rest, so Bess and Lexa arranged to go to Vence the following afternoon.

Somehow the whole day slipped past as they talked in the rooftop garden. Looking at her watch, Lexa gasped when she saw that it was after seven.

'I'll have to go,' she said with an amazed smile.

'Stay for dinner,' Bess and Clea echoed at exactly the same time. 'You won't be putting us out, we always cook extra in case somebody drops in,' Clea added, seeing her doubt.

'Thank you,' Lexa smiled. 'But you must all come and eat with me very soon.'

'We will,' Bess assured her, laughing.

They ate dinner inside, in the large dining room. The walls were white, hung with richly-patterned weavings in bright colours. Huge earthenware pots stood on the polished wooden floorboards. Clea had made them; she was a potter by trade. They were quite beautiful and Lexa could not help remarking on them.

Larry had brought home an intense young Frenchman called Pierre, an artist like Larry himself, and the conversation was lively, stimulating. The whole atmosphere of the house was relaxed, untidy and friendly, and Lexa felt quite sad when it was time for her to leave.

'Don't forget tomorrow,' Bess reminded her as she left.

She arrived back at the villa very late. The telephone was ringing as she opened the door. It was Rex, and she chatted to him for ten minutes before taking a shower and going to bed, feeling exhausted but happy.

It was good to have company, but she was glad to be alone at the villa, at least for a few days, until Zack got back.

Her life in London was packed and rushed. She hardly ever seemed to have a minute to herself. She had needed this holiday alone to sort herself out, to think about herself and the future, to renew her energy resources, recharge her batteries. It was so quiet and peaceful. She fell asleep almost immediately.

As soon as she woke the next morning, she knew exactly what she wanted to do. She pulled on her bikini and went for a swim in the pool, gasping as she dived in. She swam a quick four lengths in the blue water, then made herself coffee and ate an orange.

The sun was hot, and after her breakfast she lay down on one of the striped sunloungers and concentrated on getting a tan, closing her eyes against the fierce glare.

As she lay there, she let her mind wander, not thinking of anything in particular, not having to talk. It was bliss.

She removed her bikini top, wanting an even, unbroken tan. There was nobody to see her, after all.

She lay on her back and relaxed, a sigh of pure pleasure escaping her.

She would sunbathe until lunch, then later she would be meeting Bess. The day stretched ahead of her, full of slow pleasures. She closed her eyes again, lazily running her fingers through her hair.

She was totally unaware of the tall powerful figure approaching her, until his shadow fell across her almost-naked body.

Her heart leapt into her throat with fear and her eyes snapped open, only to find herself staring at Jase.

CHAPTER EIGHT

For a few seconds, Lexa was totally paralysed, staring up into his lean, fiercely attractive face.

'Hello Lexa.' His voice was low, husky, and her nerve endings tingled with awareness.

His narrowed golden gaze slid over her, lingering on her bare tautening breasts, her long smooth legs.

'You!' she gasped, still reeling with shock, and realising her nakedness, the probing of his eyes on her breasts, sat up jerkily and reached for her bikini top, her fingers trembling and clumsy as she tried to fasten it.

'Allow me.' Smiling slightly, Jase deftly clipped it together, his cool fingers lightly brushing her bare skin and making her quiver violently.

'What are you doing here?' she demanded, cursing the revealing blush on her cheeks. 'I spoke to Rex last night on the phone, and he mentioned nothing about you coming here.'

'Perhaps Rex didn't know,' Jase told her laconically, then shook his head. 'I see you haven't lost your touch—you still know how to make a guy feel really welcome, my love.'

'Do you expect me to make you welcome?' she demanded scornfully, still too stunned by his appearance to be anything other than defensive.

'Why not?' He stood in front of her, legs slightly apart. She could feel his eyes on her face, on her body and wished that her bikini was not so small or so revealing. She was silent.

She had the urge to run, but shock at seeing him again after all this time held her perfectly still, and she could not help herself glancing covertly up at him through her thick veiling lashes.

He had not changed at all. He was probably more magnificent than she remembered. His dark hair was longer, perhaps, thick and vital against his neck. He looked tired.

She let her eyes slide over his strongly-defined face and powerful body, the old hunger gripping her like a vice.

'You haven't changed,' Jase said quietly, though she could read no expression, no emphasis in the words. 'How have you been, Lexa?'

'I've been fine.' She was amazed at how cool, how distant she sounded. Turning her face away from him, she reached for the dark glasses nearby and slid them on to her nose, a kind of protection, a shield against him.

Her mind was reeling, her thoughts in total chaos, but her small face revealed nothing of her confusion, a trick she had learned to perfection over the past year.

She lay back on the sunlounger, her body still and nervous, not even looking at him, pretending that he was not even there. She could still feel his eyes sliding over her smooth bare limbs, but held herself rigid, determined that he would not know how she really felt. Out of the corner of her eye she saw him impatiently rake a hand through his thick black hair. He seemed about to say something, but then, without a word, turned on his heel and disappeared inside the villa.

Lexa let out a long shaken breath and closed her eyes. What was he doing here? Why did she have to meet him again after all this time? Was he staying?

She did not think she could bear to stay in the villa

with him, yet what choice did she have? She supposed she could always go to Cannes and find Zack, stay with him. She knew he would not mind, in fact she knew he would welcome her. One thing was certain—her peaceful holiday was completely and utterly ruined.

She sat up, reaching for her cigarettes, unable to keep still for a moment longer. She felt restless and uneasy. Lighting a cigarette, she inhaled on it deeply, knowing the painful contraction of her heart as she thought about Jase.

She ached with love for him; she had known the second she saw him that none of her love had died or faded, it was probably stronger, deeper than it had been at their last encounter. How depressing that was! She pushed her soft curls out of her eyes, wondering what to do, and a thought crept irrelevantly, treacherously into her mind.

It was so good to see Jase again. She had been waiting and waiting, dreaming for twelve long months of the moment when she would see his hard, devastatingly attractive face again, and her heart leapt, beating heavily in her ears at the thought that he was only a few yards away, inside the villa.

Then she thought of how she had betrayed herself, made such a fool of herself, the last time they had been together, and sighed, that tiny worm of embarrassment curling inside her again, strengthening her defences.

Every time she looked at him, she would be thinking of that, imagining that he was thinking about it too. Her pride came to her rescue, stiffening her spine as she stubbed out her cigarette.

She had faced him when he arrived, she could do it again. She would be cool and collected and he would have no idea what was going on inside her head.

It was the only way she could survive, if he was intending to stay.

She strained her ears for sounds of movement or activity inside the villa, but there was total silence. Lexa stood up, stretching, and crept inside, her bare feet making no noise on the cold tiled floors. The lounge was empty, as was the kitchen. There was no sign of Jase anywhere. Perhaps he'd gone. She hurried to open the front door, her heart sinking as she saw the low black Porsche parked next to her white hire car.

She shut the door again quickly, and turning, noticed one of the bedroom doors slightly ajar. Silently creeping towards it, she knocked lightly. No answer.

Pushing it open, she tentatively stuck her head round. In the cool dimness, she could see Jase sprawled on the bed, lying on his back, one arm flung out, the other behind his head. His deep peaceful breathing signified that he was asleep, and Lexa crept nearer, drawn by something inside her that she did not examine too closely.

His hair was wet from the shower, his shirt open, revealing the hard lines of his hair-roughened chest, the muscular flatness of his stomach. Lexa stared down at him, emotion twisting blindly inside her. His face was relaxed, lips slightly parted, and she ached to touch him. It gave her intense pleasure just to look at him.

She felt the hot helpless tears flooding her eyes and left the room before she gave away her presence and woke him.

She dressed carelessly for her sight-seeing trip with Bess, pulling on tight jeans and a white sleeveless blouse, checking her face in the mirror to make sure that her eyes were not still swollen from crying. Bess was picking her up at the villa because it was on the right road for Vence and there was no point in taking two cars. Lexa was ready early, pacing around restlessly, the villa suddenly a prison from which there was no escape.

She made some coffee, unable to face the thought of any lunch, late though it was. The whole day seemed to have slipped by while she had been struggling with the emotions induced by seeing Jase again. Making the coffee wasted ten minutes and as she sipped it slowly, she wondered how she would cope.

Her pride told her that she could not run away: to do that would be admitting everything she was desperately trying to hide. She had to face the unpalatable fact that she would be seeing Jase all her life. He was her stepbrother, after all, and family ties and commitments were bound to throw them together again and again. She wouldn't always be in a position to run away every time he came within talking distance, she had to accept that right now. The only thing to do was to stay, to use this enforced period together as a testing time.

He would never love her, she had accepted that with as much difficulty as she had accepted the fact that she would never stop loving him. But he would never know that, she wanted him to think that she had got over her 'crush' on him.

She would treat him politely, carefully, and perhaps, if she tried hard enough, they would be able to get on reasonably, superficially well.

She washed her coffee cup, not fighting the desolation that swept over her. Was this all she had to look forward to, she asked herself wearily, barely getting on with Jase, when she loved him so desperately?

The doorbell made her jump and she hurried into the hall, grabbing her handbag, hoping that the noise would not wake him.

Bess stood outside, smiling. 'Ready?' Lexa nodded, pulling the door closed as quietly as she could.

Bess was staring at the black Porsche. 'That's some car.'

'It belongs to my stepbrother, Jase. . . . He arrived this morning,' Lexa explained, trying to sound casual even though she stumbled over his name.

'Very nice,' Bess smiled as the climbed into her car.

The afternoon passed very pleasantly, although Lexa couldn't get Jase out of her thoughts for a single second.

As soon as they arrived in Vence, they found a streetside café and ordered long cold drinks. It was an old market town, Bess read from her guide, founded by the Romans, and still enclosed by ancient walls.

They visited the Cathedral and the Chapelle de la Rosaire, decorated by Matisse, then spent the rest of their time browsing round the shops and the many art galleries in the town.

Lexa's feet were hot and aching by the time they returned to the car, but her desolate mood had vanished, helped by Bess's friendliness and the beauty of her surroundings.

The sun was fading slightly as they drove back towards Nice. The hills around Vence were covered with flowers, specially cultivated, scenting the air, brightly colouring the dark earth. They were beautiful, and yet Lexa stared at them blindly, almost dreading the fast approaching moment when they arrived back at the villa and she would have to face Jase again. Perhaps he'll be out, she told herself, trying to stay calm. She couldn't imagine him waiting in for her. She started chatting brightly to Bess in an effort to block out these disturbing thoughts.

All too soon the villa came into sight, as the car rounded a steep bend.

'Would you like to come in for a drink? You could stay for dinner,' she said, in a strange nervousness clutching at her stomach at the thought of going inside alone.

Bess smiled regretfully. 'I'd love to, but I'm expecting a phone call and I have a date with an old friend later.'

'Some other time, perhaps,' said Lexa with cheerful dismay.

'Yes, I'd like that.'

The car pulled to a halt and Lexa slowly got out.

'I'll see you soon,' said Bess, switching on the engine. 'Thanks for a lovely afternoon.'

'I enjoyed it. See you!' Lexa slammed the door and waved as the car shot off.

She walked towards the front door on legs that felt as weak as water. There was music coming from the lounge and she walked in, knowing that she could not escape.

Jase was on the telephone, talking in rapid French, his voice low, laughing.

Lexa flung herself down on one of the couches, kicking off her sandals, trying not to listen to his conversation even though she suspected that he was talking to a woman, and jealousy was searing through her. She watched him surreptitiously. The lines of tiredness had gone from his face, he looked alert and relaxed. He was wearing old jeans and a dark blue shirt, his powerful body easy and graceful as he talked.

She looked down at the hands twisting nervously in her lap and deliberately stilled them, not wanting him to notice her nervousness. Finally he replaced the receiver and turned to her with a slightly guarded smile. 'Enjoy your afternoon?' His eyes flicked over her, immediately noting her tense still hands.

'Sightseeing,' she replied briefly. 'We went to Vence.'

Jase lit a cigarette and coiled himself into one of the chairs opposite her. 'I'm afraid I slept all afternoon.' He shook his head wryly. 'I went out like a light.'

'You looked tired,' she said nervously.

'I'd been driving all night. Would you like a drink?'

She nodded. 'Whisky, please.' Her voice was cool and she veiled her hungry eyes with her lashes, watching every movement he made, her face hot every time he looked at her.

He poured out two measures of whisky and added ice, handing one to her, returning to his seat.

'It's been a long time,' he said softly, watching her through narrowed eyes. 'It's good to see you again.'

Lexa's eyes dropped and she felt her heart pounding. It was good to see him, but she had no intention of telling him so.

'Yes, it has been a long time,' she agreed coolly. 'Are you staying?'

'Would it be inconvenient for you?' he asked expressionlessly.

'Zack is working in Cannes. He should be back by the end of the week,' she replied shortly.

Jase's dark brows rose. 'Are you trying to tell me something, my love?' She flushed.

'I don't know what you mean.'

'No? How are things with you and Zack Harvey?' he asked softly.

'Everything is fine. We're very close,' she added recklessly.

'Close? You're lovers?'

'I . . . that's none of your business.' Lexa took a large gulp of her drink and coughed as it hit the back of her throat.

'I'll take it that you're not, as you've been using separate rooms here.' He smiled at her.

'Very clever,' she retorted coldly, realising that whatever impression she had been hoping to give him had backfired. She hated his perception. 'Been snooping, Jase?'

He laughed. 'I don't have to—I can see it in your beautiful eyes.'

'Then you'll also see that I object to your personal questions,' she snapped. It was the same as it always had been between them. They had never indulged in polite small talk, it had always been straight to the point, however brutal, however hurtful. She did not know why. She could talk for hours about nothing in particular with everybody but Jase.

'Put it down to friendly interest,' he drawled coolly.

Lexa nervously licked her lips. 'Why have you come here?' she asked directly, changing the subject. She had been wondering ever since he walked in on her this morning.

'Let's say I'm here on an errand of mercy.'

His reply was cryptic, making absolutely no sense to her, but she did not question him further. He clearly had no intention of explaining himself and she would not give him the satisfaction of knowing her curiosity. She fell silent, concentrating on her drink and trying to think up a feasible excuse to escape from the room.

Jase was staring at her, she could almost feel the probe of his shrewd golden eyes.

'Can I take it that Zack Harvey had replaced Nick in your affections?' he asked suddenly, very softly.

Lexa's head jerked up, her eyes meeting his for one explosive second before she lowered her lashes. Why was he asking all these questions about Zack?

'Nick's in America,' she answered evasively.

'And you don't give a damn.'

'I always told you the truth about Nick,' she said stonily.

She heard him sigh heavily, unaware that his next words were going to be a bombshell.

'I know. And I owe you an apology for the things I said about you and him. I know now that you were never lovers.'

Lexa stared at him, open-mouthed with surprise. 'How? How do you know?' She could hardly believe her ears.

Jase's mouth twisted. 'Nick told me.'

'When?'

'We met in New York when he was playing there a month or so ago. I misjudged you, Lexa, and I can only say that I'm very sorry. I have no excuse to offer—none that you'd accept, anyway.'

'You believed him, but you never believed me,' she said sadly.

'No, I didn't believe you,' Jase admitted wryly. 'At the time, it all seemed to fit and I . . . oh, what the hell, it's too late now for post-mortems. I just wanted you to know that I'm sorry.'

'It doesn't matter, as long as you know the truth,' she said generously. 'The worst thing was that you thought I didn't care about Rex and. . . .' She broke off abruptly. What was the point in raking over these old ashes? Whether or not he had ever believed she and Nick to be lovers did not change the fact that he did not love her, and that was all that really mattered. As Jase said, it was too late for post-mortems.

'I know.' His voice was tinged with weariness. 'Forgive me, Lexa.'

She lifted her eyes to his, the emerald depths gentle, not blaming, but forgiving. She had forgiven him long ago.

She heard the hiss of his indrawn breath, then their

eyes locked, holding for long sweet seconds until he broke the contact.

'Have you eaten?' he asked softly. Lexa shook her head, her heart turning over at the warmth in his smile.

'Can I buy you dinner?'

She shook her head again. 'I'm too tired to go out. We walked round Vence until my feet felt as though they were dropping off. I might take you up on that offer another time.'

Jase smiled. 'Are you hungry?'

'Ravenous!'

'I'll make something for us both.' He got to his feet with easy grace. 'You can relax,' he added teasingly as she tried to struggle out of her chair. She did as she was told, sinking down again as he disappeared into the kitchen.

She could hear him whistling as he worked and she smiled, realising for the first time just how much she had missed him. It had been like having a part of herself torn out when he left. Now he was back, and for a little while at least, she was whole again.

Jase prepared cold roast chicken, salad and hot jacket potatoes for them both and produced a bottle of chilled wine. They ate on the terrace, and although she tried not to, Lexa could not help comparing this meal to the one she had shared with Zack two days ago, in exactly the same place at almost exactly the same time. She had enjoyed her meal with Zack, but this meal with Jase was totally different, sparkling somehow. He made her laugh, holding her completely in his power as he talked. Lexa was spellbound, intensely alive to every word he spoke, every indolent movement of his body, every lazy look he gave her, falling under the magnetic spell of his charm, his forceful personality, his gentleness, as deeply as she always had done.

The wine, too, relaxed her careful guard, making her forget her promise to herself to hold him coldly at arm's length.

Later, as she happily carried the dishes to the kitchen, she was suddenly startled by an enormous moth flying blindly into her face, its soft wings beating frantically against her cheek. She cried out involuntarily, and the dishes fell from her hands, smashing into hundreds of noisy pieces on the tiled floor.

Jase was beside her within a split second. 'What is it?' His hands closed urgently on her bare shoulders.

'A moth,' she whispered, feeling very silly.

His long fingers burned against her skin. They were moving, sliding beneath her thin blouse, gently stroking the hollows beneath her collarbone. He smiled at her, his eyes dark, very serious. 'My poor frightened love,' he said softly, huskily, and his head bent nearer.

Their mouths touched gently, as he brushed her lips with his own. He felt the tremor that ran through her and pulled her against his hard body, his arms coming around her like bands of steel, his kiss deepening, his mouth parting hers with hungry expertise.

Of their own volition, Lexa's arms crept up around his neck, her small hands tangling in his thick hair. It was as though they had never been apart, and she responded desperately, unable to resist him, her love was so deep.

Jase was breathing unevenly, his mouth trailing over her face, kissing her eyes, scorching where it touched. The desire that she had suppressed so fiercely for a year rose up in her at his touch, totally engulfing her as she leant weakly against him.

His hands found the buttons of her blouse, quickly undoing them, and he groaned as he found the soft warm skin beneath.

He stared into her eyes, his own glazed with aroused passion. 'I want you, Lexa,' he muttered huskily, his voice very deep, liquid. 'You've no idea how much I want you. I've waited a year to touch you again, dreaming, imagining, *aching* for this moment.'

His mouth touched her forehead, her cheeks, finally brushing her lips with aching slowness, until she whispered his name, pulling him closer, and he took full possession of her mouth once more.

His long hard fingers were moving on her body, gently stroking her warm bare flesh, moving upwards, closing on the firm softness of her breasts, his fingertips delicately brushing over her stiff nipples, until she moaned, deep in her throat, her own hands clenching against his shoulders, sharp pleasure searing through her.

She fumbled with the buttons of his shirt until his powerful chest was bare beneath her seeking fingers. She touched him, totally beyond coherent thought now, knowing only her desire, her need for him.

His skin was smooth, warm, the muscles beneath tense and unyielding. Lexa ran her fingers through the fine hair that matted his chest until she felt him shudder and his arms tightened around her in a sudden convulsive movement, holding her closely, their bodies coming together, her breasts aching against the roughness of his bare chest.

He kissed her again and she could tell by the clenched hardness of his body that he was fully aroused. She pressed herself closer, her mouth moving beneath his.

It took some seconds for the harsh insistent ringing of the telephone to filter through into her brain. As it did, she stiffened in Jase's arms, a cold clear sanity returning.

'Jase, the phone,' she whispered against his mouth.

'Ignore it,' he murmured thickly.

But Lexa couldn't. She felt sick at what she had nearly allowed to happen between them. Jase would now know for sure that she still loved him. Taking him by surprise, she tore herself out of his arms and moved with lightning speed towards the telephone, her fingers shaking so much that she could not even manage to button her blouse, having to hold it together as she picked up the receiver.

It was a woman, she was speaking before Lexa had a chance to say a word. 'Jase darling, what took you so long?'

Lexa froze, her mind numbing, as she listened to that low, laughing, intimate voice.

'Hold the line, please,' she said in a flat toneless whisper. She turned round and found Jase leaning in the doorway, his shirt still hanging open, exposing his hard brown chest, his eyes still dark with desire as he looked at her.

'For you,' she said very quietly, her emerald eyes blank, her hand still clutching the edges of her blouse together.

Jase swore under his breath, moving slowly forward. 'Who is it?'

'I've no idea.' She was in the grip of a fragile, icy calm. She walked out of the room as he picked up the receiver. She could not bear to hear him talking to that laughing woman, she could not bear to stay in the same room as him. She walked into her bedroom and shut the door, locking it from the inside. She moved across the room in a daze and sat down at the dressing table, staring with blind eyes at the reflection in the mirror.

She examined her feelings in an almost detached way. Love, jealousy, self-disgust, desire—she could still feel the desire aching in her stomach, desperate for release. Jase had been here for less than a day and already she had made a fool of herself, repeating all the old patterns that she thought, hoped were broken. It was the same as it had always been. He only had to touch her and she melted into his arms.

She supposed she ought to thank that unknown, undoubtedly beautiful woman for her timely interruption of their lovemaking. Despite her stabbing jealousy, she knew that had the phone not rung, she would have been in Jase's bed by now, with no thought of denying him or herself.

She shivered, despite the heat of the night, hardly recognising the woman who stared back at her from the mirror. Her hair was tousled, where Jase had run his fingers so urgently through it, her lips swollen, her blouse still hanging open exposing taut aching breasts, her eyes clouded, pained.

She turned away, not wanting to look at herself, and jumped like a scared rabbit when Jase tapped lightly on the door, impatiently rattling the handle when he found it locked.

'Go away,' she heard herself say in a cold firm voice that was at total odds with her feelings.

'Lexa, open this door, I want to talk to you!' he called with angry patience.

Talk? She almost laughed. Talking was the last thing on both their minds! 'I'm going to bed – go away!'

'Lexa, if you don't open this door, so help me, I'll kick it down!' It was no idle threat and she knew he had the strength to do it.

Defeated, she fastened her blouse, her fingers still shaking, and walked slowly towards the door, releasing the lock and stepping back as he came in. He seemed to fill the room with his angry masculine presence and she stared up into his face with huge eyes, visibly jumping as he took a step towards her.

'Lexa, you're not frightened of me?' There was surprise in his voice, wiping out his impatience. All traces of his desire for her seemed to have gone, his face was an expressionless mask, his eyes unfathomable.

'I'm tired,' she replied evasively. It was partly the truth, she felt exhausted, both physically and emotionally, but she was frightened, not of Jase, but of herself and the realisation that her feelings for him could lead her into all kinds of trouble.

'Lexa, I won't hurt you, I won't force you to do anything you don't want to do—you should know that.' He had misunderstood her reactions, he still thought that she was afraid of him. His mouth twisted self-deprecatingly. 'I guess I lost control just now——'

'Don't apologise, please!' she cut in urgently. She could not bear him to feel bad about those beautiful moments she had spent in his arms.

'I wasn't going to.' Jase smiled, and bending his dark head, tenderly kissed her mouth. 'Goodnight, my love.' He walked out of the room, quietly closing the door behind him.

Lexa stared after him for long moments, her eyes blind on the wooden door, a faint smile curving her mouth. Then she washed and went to bed.

She woke in the middle of the night, abrupt and anxious. She lay gazing into the darkness, not knowing what had woken her—probably some dark disturbing dream that she had already forgotten. She looked at her watch. It was after two. She wondered if Jase was asleep, and a feeling of loneliness washed over her, a desire to be near him.

She turned over on to her side and tried to get back to sleep. She couldn't; she was wide awake, restless. She slid out of bed and crept into the hall. The light was still on in the lounge and as she peeped in, she saw Jase, working, signing papers from the thick sheaf in front of him.

She stood watching him for ages, until, sensing her presence, he slowly turned his head and saw her.

'What's the matter?' he asked softly.

Lexa took a tentative step into the room, feeling embarrassed. She saw his eyes narrowing on her body, barely veiled by the thin silk of her nightdress.

'I can't sleep,' she explained, biting her lower lip.

'Neither can I.' His voice was rough and she knew that he was thinking of their lovemaking. Then, surprisingly he smiled. 'I guess I shouldn't have slept the afternoon away. Do you want a drink? That might help.'

I want you, she longed to say. 'No, thanks.' Her voice was a small sigh and she shifted from one foot to the other, thinking that she was mad to have come in here. She sat down on the end of the couch he was sitting on. 'I don't want to interrupt your work—please carry on. I'll just sit here for a while.'

Jase smiled at her solemn face. 'Okay.' He returned his attention to his work, and glancing at him from the corner of her eye, Lexa felt strangely piqued.

She sat gazing into space, desperately aware of him next to her. In the silence she could hear him breathing if she held her own breath and strained her ears. She moved a little nearer to him, making herself more comfortable. Jase looked at her, his golden eyes amused, tender, and suddenly slid an arm around her shoulders, hugging her against his hard relaxed body. Lexa laid her head on his shoulder, turning her face into his throat, feeling utterly content, her eyelids drooping. She fell asleep almost immediately and Jase held her, staring down at her, keeping perfectly still so as not to disturb her, his expression unreadable.

Some time later he lifted her into his arms and carried her to her bed, pulling the covers over her and gently kissing her mouth before switching off the light and quietly leaving the room.

CHAPTER NINE

MID-AFTERNOON, two days later, Lexa arrived back at the villa after having lunch with Bess and Clea. She felt happy, singing as she parked the car next to Jase's black Porsche. Things had been going well between Jase and herself, although she had not seen much of him. He had been out all the previous day, not getting back until after she was asleep. He was probably spending his time with the woman who had telephoned him, Lexa thought, sour with jealousy. She had not asked him, though.

They were friendly when they were together, if a little wary of each other. Jase was holding back, treating her carefully, not pushing her, and Lexa was well pleased with the way she was managing to stay outwardly cool in his company, keeping him at a relatively safe distance.

The other good news was that Zack was expected back that evening, and as a sort of welcome home for him and the other men, Lexa had arranged a small party at the villa, inviting Clea and Larry, Bess and Jean-Paul and Bruce. It was to be a surprise. She had only thought of it over lunch, so there were lots of preparations to be made.

She hurried inside, barely able to manage the huge box of groceries she had bought in Nice. She had everything worked out and intended to spend the afternoon baking and preparing the food for the party. First she would take a swim in the pool, she decided, longing for the freedom of the cool water. She dumped the groceries in the kitchen, wiping away the slight film of perspiration that her exertions had produced.

She had to find Jase and tell him about the party. She knew he wouldn't mind.

She heard noise, quiet talking, music, issuing from the lounge, and went in, the excited words dying on her lips as her eyes registered the scene before her.

She stopped dead in her tracks, the hiss of her indrawn breath turning the heads of the other two people in the room.

Lexa stared and stared, hardly able to believe what she saw. Jase stood by the window, his arms around Eva Sutherland, her arms around his waist, her auburn head bent to his wide shoulder with intimate familiarity. It was too great a coincidence, and it hit her like a kick in the stomach, leaving her breathless, hurting, as she realised that Eva Sutherland was Nick's ex-girl-friend, the woman he loved, the woman Jase had stolen from his brother.

It all fitted. Clea and Larry were old friends of Zack's, and Zack was one of Nick's best friends. They all knew each other, a close circle of friends.

I should have realised before, Lexa thought dazedly, as soon as I saw her. Eva is hardly a common name. Drawing on sheer will-power, she came to her senses, moving and thinking mechanically as the silence built up in the room. Eva was smiling slightly, obviously surprised, while Jase was staring at Lexa, easily reading her expression, a frown pulling together his dark brows.

'Lexa. . . .' he began almost impatiently, but she didn't give him time to speak.

'I . . . I'm sorry, I didn't mean to . . . to barge in. . . .' she mumbled, red-faced, turning to go.

'Don't be ridiculous, you haven't barged in on anything.' Jase slowly released Eva from his arms. Lexa could see that the other girl had been crying. 'Let me introduce you——'

'We've already met,' Lexa cut in quickly, somehow managing a slight smile at Eva.

'Yes, Lexa came for lunch at Clea's a few days ago,' Eva explained calmly, her voice friendly. 'I had no idea you were staying with Jase.' Her eyes were very curious as they rested on Lexa, and Lexa smiled. She could almost read Eva's thoughts. She was wondering exactly what was going on with Lexa and Jase. She was worried.

'Jase is my stepbrother,' Lexa enlightened her with a tight smile, ignoring Jase completely.

'Ah!' The relief on the other woman's face was almost visible. 'That's quite a coincidence.'

'Yes, isn't it?' Lexa could not completely hide her bitterness. She was remembering things that Nick had said about Eva and Jase, things that she thought she had forgotten, *wished* she had forgotten.

'It's a lovely place,' Eva smiled, looking round. She was being polite.

'Yes.' Lexa was abrupt and she did not dare to look at Jase. She felt as though she was having a terrible nightmare. All she wanted to do was wake up.

Jase was fixing drinks, leaving them to it. 'What will you have?' he asked her as he passed Eva a cool looking glass, tinkling with ice.

'Nothing for me, thanks.' Her voice was too bright. 'I've got a thousand things to do. I only came in to tell you that I'm having a small party tonight—you're both invited, of course.'

'Thank you, I'll look forward to it,' Eva accepted immediately, and Lexa felt her fists clenching behind her back.

Jase was silent and she could not wait for his answer.

She had to get out of that room before she screamed. She had just realised that it had been Eva on the telephone two nights before. 'Jase, darling' she had called him.

'Please excuse me, I have lots to do for tonight.' She turned towards the door, her heart clenching with pain.

'Can I help?'

Lexa closed her eyes as Eva spoke. Why did the other girl have to be so friendly, so pleasant? 'No, I can manage ... thanks for the offer, though.' She did not look back as she left the room, her politeness to Eva almost killing her. She practically ran into the kitchen, she was so anxious to get away from them.

She leant against the sink, covering her face with her hands. She could hear Eva laughing in the lounge and she felt like grinding her teeth together. Her mind tormented her with the picture of them wrapped in each other's arms, as she walked in on them.

'Lexa, are you all right?' Jase was suddenly behind her, turning her to face him, his touch gentle, impersonal, yet setting her skin on fire.

'Of course I am.' She shrugged free of his touch. 'I think I've been out in the sun too much,' she added by way of an explanation for her odd behaviour.

Jase's eyes searched her face. 'Sure?'

She nodded mutely, wanting him to go.

'You know who Eva is, don't you?' His voice was calm, unworried.

'It's none of my business,' she said desperately. The very last person she wanted to talk about was Eva.

'Lexa, you don't think ...?'

'Please, Jase, I'm very busy.' Her voice was cold, devoid of emotion, and her emerald eyes told him to go. His mouth tightened as he looked into her face, but he walked back into the lounge without a word.

Lexa threw herself into the preparations for the party, working hard all afternoon. And while she worked, her mind was racing, her hands working automatically. She knew now why Jase had come to France. He was here to see Eva, which meant that he had lied to Nick when he told him that he did not know where Eva was, had lied when he'd said he was not seeing her. Their affair was obviously going strong even after all this time, and at least he had not abandoned her as Nick had thought.

Perhaps that was why Jase had not yet married. If he married Eva, there was no saying what Nick might do. One thing was certain, it would tear the family apart and Rex would be very badly hurt by the whole sordid business. At least Jase had had the decency to spare his father that. And then with a staggering flash of pain, Lexa remembered that Eva had been pregnant when she and Nick had split up.

Feeling sick, she sank on to a chair, her legs not holding her. Eva had borne Jase's child. The words rang in her head. Deep in her heart she now realised that she had still been cherishing some tiny hope that Jase would come to love her, that everything would be worked out between them, She realised it now because that hope had just been killed. In the end, Jase would marry Eva; he was lost to Lexa for ever.

Somehow, she got to her feet and carried on with her baking. Where was the child? she wondered. Eva was in Nice alone, of that she was sure. Why hadn't she brought the child with her when she knew Jase was to be here? Was it a girl or a boy? Did it look like Jase? So many unanswered questions, questions that she could not ask. Sighing, she decided that she probably did not want to know the answers anyway. Jase had acted honourably and perhaps the love between him and Eva had just happened, perhaps they hadn't been able to help themselves. She knew that Jase would not have deliberately hurt Nick.

And he had not abandoned Eva, presumably he had taken responsibility for the child. When Nick finally got over Eva, Lexa felt sure that Jase and Eva would marry. Which leaves me totally alone, she thought desolately, in love with a man who loves somebody else. She felt the tears of self-pity blocking her throat and with will power she had not known existed inside herself until today, swallowed them back and carried on working. She had been without Jase for most of her life, what did another fifty or so years matter? she asked herself hysterically.

Zack arrived at six. Lexa was lying out by the pool, the preparations for the party finally finished. She was pretending to be reading a book. Eva and Jase were still in the lounge, she supposed, though she had neither seen or heard anything of them.

She did not hear Zack's car pulling up and only his shouted greeting brought her head round. She felt desperately pleased to see him, and flung her arms around him, kissing him.

He kissed her back, smiling. 'Don't tell me you missed me!' he teased.

'Like mad,' she replied, laughing. Zack was her friend, she was not so alone here now.

'Whose is the black Porsche?'

'It belongs to Jase, he's staying here, Lexa explained briefly, her face flushing.

'Well, what a surprise—I haven't seen him for years!' Zack looked pleased.

'He's the same as ever,' she said flatly. 'And talking of surprises, I've got one for you. I'm throwing a welcome back party for you tonight and I need some help buying the drinks, so as soon as you've had time to catch your breath, you can drive into Nice with me and give me a hand.' She kissed his cheek persuasively.

'Sure. I'm ready when you are,' he laughed, and swung her into his arms. 'A party? What a sweet, wonderful girl you are!' His mouth found hers and he began kissing her. Lexa found herself responding, wanting it to be right because she felt so alone, her mouth moving beneath his.

Zack's arms tightened at her response and with his actions she realised what she was doing, and broke away, filled with self-disgust. How could she use Zack like this? Her mind was so confused after the events of the day that she did not know what she was doing. As she was about to apologise, her eyes suddenly met Jase's. He was standing right behind them, neither had heard his silent approach. His face was frozen, his eyes cold and hard.

She stiffened in Zack's arms, turning crimson with embarrassment, cringing at the contempt she saw in Jase. Zack turned too, then, his face breaking into a smile. 'Jase! Great to see you.' He held out his hand. 'Lexa told me you were here.'

'Did she indeed?' Jase's eyes mocked her, as he took Zack's hand.

'I'll go and change,' she said quickly to Zack, and disappeared inside as fast as she could, wondering where Eva was and wondering what on earth was the matter with Jase.

The party was a great success, Lexa knew, as she made her way to the kitchen to fetch more wine from the refrigerator. Everybody except herself seemed to be enjoying themselves, the music and laughter following her into the empty room. But she felt exhausted with the effort of appearing bright and in the party mood.

She slammed the refrigerator shut too violently and carried the wine back to the party, pinning an over-bright smile on to her face as she re-entered the lounge. She spent the next hour chatting to Bess and dancing with Zack and Bruce, her eyes and attention riveted on Jase the whole while. She watched him dance with Eva, watched him laughing with Jean-Paul, her heart aching as she turned away.

'That stepbrother of yours is really something,' Bess remarked, her eyes following him as well.

'Yes, I suppose he is.' Lexa tried to sound noncommittal, uncaring.

'You suppose? I'd say it was a fact.' Bess laughed as Jean-Paul claimed her for a dance. 'You don't know how lucky you are!'

Lucky? Lexa shook her head, moving across the room to check the food. The perfect hostess, she thought bitterly. Halfway across, a hand closed on her arm.

She turned smiling. 'Dance with me,' Jase ordered softly.

Her smile faded. 'I have to check. . . .' Before her excuse was uttered, she was pulled into his arms. The music was slow and sensual, all of a sudden, as though he had planned it that way. She tried to pull away, her heart racing, angry yet exhilarated by his possessive touch, but his arms were too strong, he held her too closely, his hands on her narrow waist, their bodies almost touching, his hard thigh brushing hers as they moved, his mouth against her hair. Bitter-sweet sensations swept through her and she could not fight him, but gave herself up to the intense pleasure of his nearness, lifting her small hands to his wide shoulders, with a sigh of acquiescence.

'You've been avoiding me all night,' he murmured against her forehead.

'No, I haven't.'

'Liar! Every time I've come within five yards, you've shot away like a scalded cat.'

'I've been busy,' she protested hastily.

Jase laughed and pulled her even closer. 'I wonder!'

Lexa ignored that, resting her cheek against his throat, breathing in the clean male scent of his skin, her whole body longing for him so fiercely that she felt dazed.

His heart was beating fast, she realised, as fast as her own, striking against her body in a deep, hurried rhythm.

She caught Zack's eyes across the room. He was staring at her and Jase, his expression surprised, almost shocked, and that look brought Lexa to her senses.

She pulled away from Jase, putting some distance between them, even though it was only a few inches, relieved as the music stopped and Jase released her.

Eva appeared beside them within a second, staring mistily at Jase, her beautiful mouth pouting. 'Won't you dance with me now, Jase?'

His expression was polite yet unreadable as he held out his hand to her, but as Lexa moved hurriedly away, she noticed that he was not holding Eva as tightly or with such intimacy as he had held her, and that brought some relief.

She strolled out on to the terrace, needing some air. The garden beckoned, quiet and peaceful, totally empty of people with whom she had to put on a bright act. Out here, she could be herself.

Tonight there was a faint breeze from the sea, blowing her soft curls from her heated cheeks, swirling the red silk of her dress around her slim bare legs.

The pool was very still, reflecting the stars in its inky depths. Lexa was glad to get away from the noisy

warmth inside. It was sheer bliss to be alone and she
wandered through the profusion of flowers, their heavy
scent floating into the night air, and somehow the peace
and quiet seemed to slow her racing mind as she stood
beneath a gnarled old olive tree, staring down at the
lights of Nice, the dark haze of the Mediterranean.

Footsteps fell quietly behind her and she whirled
round, relieved to see Zack and not Jase, as she had
feared.

'All alone?' He came and stood beside her, not
looking at her, but gazing across the sea towards the
horizon.

'Yes, I needed some air.' Her voice sounded peculiar
even to her own ears.

'Great party,' he remarked brightly. She nodded in
silent agreement, feeling the strain, the tension between
them. They were talking like shy strangers, and
unfortunately, she knew what it was all about.

'So what's your excuse for being out here, missing all
the fun?' she asked teasingly, staring at the sharp
familiar lines of his profile.

'I was looking for you.'

'Don't tell me the wine has run out again.' Her
attempts at lightness were grating on her own nerves,
she couldn't even guess what they were doing to Zack.

'Lexa, will you marry me?' He spoke slowly, casually,
the question coming right out of the blue.

She was shocked into silence for a second, unable to
tell whether or not he was serious.

'Zack, I. . . .'

'You know I love you,' he said quietly, still not
looking at her, still staring out towards the horizon, the
hunch of his shoulders speaking of defeat.

It was what she had feared most. How could she have
been so blind, so stupid over the past year? An aching

sadness gripped her and she was all the more miserable because she was so fond of him, because she had never ever encouraged him.

'No, I didn't know,' she said very gently.

Zack smiled rather bitterly. 'I didn't intend to tell you. I've been playing it cool for so long, and now I've frightened you.' He ran his hand over his face. 'It was seeing you with him—he's the one, isn't he?'

It was that obvious, Lexa thought in desolation. One dance and Zack had fitted it all together.

'Yes, it's Jase,' she admitted with flat honesty. 'It always has been.'

'And I suppose that's my answer.' Zack turned and looked at her for the first time and she saw the heavy emotion in his eyes.

'I'm sorry.' It was so inadequate, but she did not know what else to say.

'So am I. I had to try—understand.'

Lexa felt the tears on her face, hating herself for not being what he wanted her to be. It was so unfair, he was so kind, so quiet and caring. Why, *why* couldn't she love him?

Jase was hard and forceful, never giving in, and yet she loved him so blindly, she could not even see Zack.

Love made such a mess of people's lives, it was so destructive. Nothing would ever be the same again between Zack and herself. She should have seen this coming, averted it somehow, instead of being so selfishly wrapped up in her own problems. If she had done that, perhaps they could have stayed friends.

As it was, she knew that Zack's declaration had changed everything between them. Now she was totally unsure, as he was, where they stood with each other, whether they would still be friends. And of course she would have to leave her job. It was as though a door had been slammed shut in her face. It was an ending of something very good.

'I understand,' she said shakily. 'Zack. . . .'

'Don't say anything else, not now.' He turned back towards the villa. 'I'll see you later.' He walked away, not waiting for any reply, and she knew that she had hurt him.

I can't help it, she wanted to shout after him. Do you think I want to love Jase? Do you think I want to hurt you? But she shouted nothing, as she watched him disappearing into the lounge, swallowed up in the noisy crowd, those stupid tears still falling down her face, feeling utterly miserable.

She turned back towards the sea, leaning her back against a tree trunk, intending to stay out all night if necessary. She could not face joining the party again.

She had no idea how long she stood alone crying, it seemed like minutes, it seemed like years, then suddenly she heard the quiet click of a lighter behind her, though she had heard nobody approaching.

The faint aroma of Turkish tobacco drifted past her, tickling her nostrils, and she knew it was Jase.

Silently, he took a few steps forward so that he stood beside her. Lexa felt his eyes on her but did not acknowledge his presence. She didn't even try to hide her tears, he could think what he liked.

Still without a word, he pulled a handkerchief from his pocket and handed it to her, then as she wiped her face and blew her nose, lit another cigarette and placed it gently between her lips. She drew on it deeply. She had not looked at him once.

'Zack Harvey has just driven off towards Nice at a breakneck speed,' he told her coolly. 'You, I find crying in the garden. What's the connection, I wonder?'

'Don't, Jase,' she whispered huskily.

'Don't? Don't what?' His jaw was tight even though his voice was cool and mocking.

'Don't be clever.' She turned her head slowly and looked into his hard face. She saw nothing there to comfort her. He did not care, how could she expect him to? He had his own problems, after all.

'I've told you before, Lexa, my love. I've given up trying to be clever with you, it always explodes right back in my face,' Jase said with soft irony.

Lexa didn't know what he was talking about and at that moment she did not particularly care, so she fell silent, watching pale petals drifting from one of the trees, watching them fall like confetti at Jase's feet.

She felt numb, subdued, in no mood to fence with him, and she felt worried about Zack. Why had he gone to Nice? Jase said he had been driving at breakneck speed. In her anxiety she could imagine him crashing the car, injuring himself. If he did, it would be her fault.

Jase watched her carefully, his eyes narrowed, assessing. 'Did he hurt you?' There was suppressed violence in the question. She shook her head numbly. 'Do you want to talk about it?' he asked gently.

Lexa sighed. 'Zack loves me,' she said simply, trusting Jase, instinctively turning to him for help.

'I knew that when I saw you together this afternoon.' There was no surprise in his voice.

'I didn't know until he told me just now.'

'Oh, Lexa, how can you be so blind where men are concerned?' He tilted up her face, caressing her jaw with his thumb, forcing her to meet his shadowed golden eyes.

'Years of practice,' she replied bitterly.

Jase smiled at her, his face tender, and she caught her breath.

'Do you love him?' His voice was low, very quiet.

'I don't know,' she heard herself saying untruthfully, perhaps wanting to hit back at him for loving Eva and not her. She was determined that he would never know how she cared for him.

'Once, you were very sure about love,' Jase said deeply, and she hated him for reminding her of that awful, humiliating scene. She had offered him everything and he had thrown it all back in her face.

Her body stiffened with a sudden flaring of anger. How did he dare to mention that now?

'You soon set me straight about that, though,' she retorted coldly. 'Schoolgirl fairytales, wasn't it?' She wasn't sure whether or not it was her imagination, but she could have sworn she saw him flinch, his eyes flickering with pain for a second. But when she looked at him again, he was as expressionless as always, his face a cold blank mask.

'You seem to have got over it, nonetheless,' he said coolly, a faint hint of questioning in his voice. Lexa felt like laughing. She had never got over him, she never would.

'Oh, yes, I got over it,' she lied. 'And at least I'll recognise infatuation if it ever hits me again. I suppose I have a lot to thank you for.'

'Lexa, there was no other way.' His voice was rough, angry.

'Please, you don't have to explain anything.' She was shivering, their conversation cutting away at her like knives.

He swore harshly. 'You're damned right I don't!'

'How boring it must be for you to have to spend so much of your time, slapping down infatuated young women!' She was icy with childish sarcasm, her temper boiling now.

Jase could be so cruel, and tonight she could not take

it. She was angry with herself over Zack and she was impotently angry with Jase because she loved him so very much and he did not give a damn. He was still hurting her and not even noticing.

She heard the hiss of his indrawn breath, his fingers bruising her as he grasped her bare shoulders. 'You crazy little bitch!' he grated savagely, his control snapping. 'Do you think it was easy for me?' He shook her until her hair fell about her face in tousled disarray and her body fell limp like a rag doll. 'I can tell you, it damned well wasn't! I wanted you more than I'd ever wanted any woman in my life before, I was aching to give you what you were asking for.' He saw the surprised fear in her wide eyes and his mouth twisted wryly. 'You didn't even know that, did you? Lexa, it was the only way to stop it dead!'

'You could have been kinder,' she flung at him stubbornly, refusing to be intimidated by his fury. They were both fiercely angry, it had happened in seconds, that savage, mercurial tension that had always bound them crackling between them like raw electricity.

'Kinder?' Jase almost shouted, his fingers tightening on the already-bruised bones of her shoulders. 'Are you crazy? Kindness would have had you in my bed faster than lightning!' He was brutally direct.

'I hate you!' Lexa hissed childishly, too angry and too humiliated to argue coherently. 'And take your hands off me, you're breaking my bones!'

Jase stared at her, his eyes flaming, out of control. 'That's the very least I'd like to do to you,' he bit out from between clenched teeth.

'It may interest you to know that I'm not at all impressed by your threats any more,' she glared, trying to still the betraying shaking of her body.

'What makes you think I want to impress

you? Believe me, sweetheart, you've got it all wrong.'
His eyes were derisive.

'Zack asked me to marry him tonight,' she said
suddenly, dropping that snippet of news like a lead
balloon.

'And?' Jase was dangerously still. He reminded her of
a tiger, stalking, ready to kill.

'And I think I'll accept,' she said recklessly.

'It will be the biggest mistake of your life.'

'You know nothing about it.' She did not even know
why she had mentioned it except that she had
instinctively known that it would make Jase angry.

'You think not?' He was very cool—too cool.

Her lips parted, ready to spit out some acid retort,
but he was too fast for her, jerking her roughly against
his powerful body, his mouth finding hers before she
had time to utter a word. That angry, hungry kiss tore
through them both like an explosion, shaking them
deeply.

Jase's mouth moved endlessly on hers with total
devastating possession, and Lexa's response was as
fierce and unbidden as his. She moaned low in her
throat as his hands loosened their punishing grip on her
shoulders, his fingers suddenly gentle, stroking, searching the yielding curves of her body.

Her own hands were trapped against his chest, she
could feel the heavy racing of his heart, His mouth left
hers, kissing her cheek, her eyes, sliding the length of
her vulnerable white throat. She clung to him,
weakened by his strength, his mastery, lost in the fire of
his lovemaking, responding mindlessly, her fingers
sliding beneath his shirt to touch his warm hair-
roughened chest, shuddering as his mouth touched hers
again and his kiss deepened hungrily.

Then, just as suddenly as he had pulled her into his

arms, he released her again, very abruptly. He moved away, his throat contracting as he swallowed, leaning his back indolently against one of the trees.

Lexa, aching for him, unable to think clearly, just stared, absently noticing that his hands were clenched stiffly at his sides, so tense that the knuckles were gleaming white with strain. He was breathing unsteadily, as she was.

'Why?' she asked sadly, as her senses came alive again, bringing with them a terrible pain.

'Jase, are you out there?' Eva's plaintive voice drifted over on the warm night air. Both ignored her, staring into each other's eyes.

'How can you marry Zack Harvey knowing how it is between you and me?' Jase asked expressionlessly.

'Is that what you were doing, trying to prove something?' Her voice was sharp with pain.

'Is that you, Jase?' Eva's voice was getting nearer.

'I didn't have to try very hard, we both know that.' The eyes that held hers were merciless, piercing her very soul.

'You swine! You've got what you want, what you stole. Why are you trying to ruin my life?' It was almost impossible to believe his callousness.

'Now, wait a minute——'

'There you both are!' Eva arrived in front of them, sensing the tension, staring from one to the other curiously. 'I've been looking all over for you. What on earth are you doing out here?' Her bright chattering voice broke between them like ice, shattering the intense moment, breaking the communication.

'I've been trying to make Lexa see sense,' Jase drawled sardonically.

Eva's fine eyebrows rose, her eyes puzzled. 'What?'

'No need to panic, Eva, he's all yours and you're

welcome to him,' said Lexa with brittle antagonism. She was well past being polite; she did not care any more. She turned on her heel and walked quickly through the garden and round the front of the villa, intending to go straight to her room without having to walk through the party.

Turning the corner, she walked straight into Zack in the darkness. 'Lexa, where are you going?' He steadied her, and she marched right past him, not saying a word. He quickly caught up with her. 'Lexa——?'

'To bed. And I'm going home in the morning. I've been here long enough,' she said calmly.

'That makes two of us. How about the early flight?'

She stopped and looked at him. 'You too?' She was glad that he was safely back from Nice, that thought, at least, pierced her numb brain.

'Me too.' He smiled crookedly. 'It's been one hell of a trip. I just want to get it over with.'

'I couldn't agree more,' she said fiercely. 'The early flight suits me fine.'

They went inside together.

CHAPTER TEN

LEXA sat slumped in front of the television, her eyes blind on the moving screen, totally unaware of what she was watching.

She had been back from Nice for a week now, and still had a little less than a week of her holiday left.

Her notice of resignation was lying on the table, neatly written, very final. She would post it tomorrow, because it would probably suit Zack better not to see her for a while.

Neither had mentioned what had happened, on the flight back to London, the last time she had seen him, but the fact that it was unspoken didn't make it any less real. She embarrassed Zack every time he looked at her, and he made her feel terribly guilty. They certainly wouldn't be able to work together again, which left her minus a special, close friend and unemployed into the bargain. She had no idea what she would do, all she knew was that she couldn't go on seeing Zack every day, reminding him of his love for her, admitted yet regretted, reminding him that she was in love with somebody else. She knew that situation inside out and she wouldn't have wished it on her worst enemy, let alone someone she was deeply fond of.

He was talking about going back to Canada for a while, so she had heard from a friend. It was probably a good idea, but it depressed Lexa terribly.

The worst mistake of her life—that was what Jase had said about her marrying Zack, and although she hated his perception she was forced to agree. It would have been a mistake, it would never have worked. She had not even really considered it, if she was honest. The whole situation was unbearable and very sad.

Lexa had not seen Jase since the night of the party—and that was something else that depressed her, that awful row they'd had. There had been something final about that as well. She buried her face in her hands. She couldn't stop thinking about him, not for a moment. Without him her life was empty.

The room grew dark around her as night fell. She did not notice that she sat in front of the noisy television, lost in thought, and when the doorbell rang, she ignored it, its insistence hardly penetrating her thoughts until it became clear that whoever was on the other side of the door had no intention of going away, their finger was jammed on the bell.

Sighing, Lexa got to her feet and walked slowly out of her flat, jumping painfully to her senses as Jase shouldered his way through the front door.

'What took you so long?' he demanded irritably.

Lexa frowned, shocked speechless, as she followed him into her flat.

'What do you think you're doing, pushing your way in here——' she began, then stopped.

He looked awful, exhausted, eyes blank and weary, mouth tight with strain, his skin pale beneath its tan. Lexa's heart clenched with sympathy as her eyes travelled over him. His powerful body was tense, the muscles rigid with a terrible strain. There was something wrong.

'Jase . . .?'

'Have you got anything to drink?' He was staring at her, unable to drag his eyes away.

'I've got some whisky.'

'That'll do fine.' He stood by the window, his mind

obviously elsewhere. She watched him for a second, then with a small gesture of impatience went into the kitchen to fetch a glass. There *was* something wrong, badly wrong, and she felt her stomach muscles tightening apprehensively, as she poured Jase a large measure of whisky.

He took it from her without a word, draining the contents of the glass in one long mouthful.

Lexa stood passively, silently aching to comfort him in some way, her love for him burning inside her. The silence lengthened until she could not bear it.

'Jase, what's the matter? What's happened?' Her voice was urgent, her eyes pleading.

He sighed heavily. 'Sit down,' he ordered gently.

Biting her lip, she did as she was told, her anxiety growing. Jase ran a hand through his dark hair, utterly weary. 'There's no easy way to tell you this. Rex is dead.'

Lexa's heart missed a beat. 'No!' She shook her head, but she knew that he was telling the truth. 'When? How?' There was a feeling of sickness clawing in her stomach.

'This afternoon. It was his heart. He was dead even before the ambulance arrived, there was nothing anybody could do,' he told her flatly. 'He was lucky to have survived that last attack, really. The doctor told me that if he'd survived this one, he would probably have been both physically and mentally damaged. Rex wouldn't have wanted to live like that, so perhaps it's better this way.'

As his words sank in Lexa felt terribly sad. She had seen Rex only two weeks ago, and he had seemed fine. 'Oh, Jase. ... ' She ran blindly into his arms and he held her tightly against his body as she began to cry.

She cried and cried, unable to believe it had happened, that she would never see Rex again. And she cried for Jase because he had lost his father and yet he was too strong to show his grief. The pain would tear him apart inside and nobody would ever know. His strong arms comforted her and he stroked back her golden hair very gently, murmuring deep soothing words that somehow comforted her.

Her tears seemed to wash some of the pain out of her system and by the time her eyes were dry, she was held by a kind of numb disbelieving acceptance of the facts. But she did not leave Jase's arms, she rested her body against his and held him as they stood together in the darkness of the room. It was very late.

'Let me stay with you tonight, Lexa,' she heard him murmur against her soft curls.

She stiffened in confusion. 'I . . . I . . . what about Eva?' she asked stupidly, not knowing if she could bear the agonising pleasure of having him so near.

'What about her?' His face was blank.

'Well, I. . . .'

'Damn Eva! Let me stay, I need you in my arms tonight.' His voice was low, intense, very weary and she could not refuse him.

'All right,' she agreed quietly, and heard him sigh.

'Thanks.'

They drank some more whisky and it helped to dull the pain, and Lexa switched on the fire because although it was early summer, the room was somehow chilled. They talked about Rex, and she watched Jase intensely, watched every gracefully-weary movement he made, loving him more than she had thought possible.

Then they went to bed. Lexa took a shower after Jase, a little embarrassed by the arrangement she had agreed to, putting off the moment when she actually had to get into bed. She brushed her hair and slid into a thin cotton nightdress edged with lace, that covered her from head to foot, then tentatively pushed open the bedroom door, her heart stopping as she saw Jase in her bed.

He had removed his shirt and was lying on his back, his hands behind his head, watching her as she nervously entered the room. She glanced hungrily at his tanned naked chest with its cloud of dark hair and at the tense heavy muscles of his arms, and her mouth went dry. How could she spend the night in his arms and not give away the fact that she was in love with him? She had been mad to agree. She skirted round the bed in a wide circle, her eyes shadowed with apprehension.

'Lexa.' He said her name softly and she nearly jumped out of her skin. His mouth tightened. 'You're not still frightened of me?'

She shook her head, the lamplight glinting in her golden hair.

'I won't touch you, I promise,' he said harshly. 'But I need to hold you tonight.'

'Why me?' she whispered, staring down at him.

'You'd really be frightened if I told you,' he taunted softly. Her eyes widened and a ghost of a smile touched his mouth. 'Because you're warm and gentle, because I remember the scent of your skin, your softness, because you're so serene—a thousand reasons, my love.'

Biting her lip, Lexa slid into bed beside him, lying stiffly at the very edge. She slowly turned her head and their eyes met as she switched out the lamp, throwing the room into darkness. Jase drew a long hard breath, one strong arm reaching for her, bringing her against the hard warmth of his body, the other curving around her so that he held her tightly, groaning softly as he buried his face in her hair.

Lexa closed her eyes, her cheek against the smooth skin of his shoulder, her own arms sliding around his waist, knowing a warm comfort at his nearness and realising that she needed him tonight as much as he needed her. Her embarrassment had completely disappeared. It was right, natural that they should hold each other in the lonely darkness of the night.

'Oh, Lexa, Lexa,' Jase whispered her name, his arms tightening. She lay still against him, in a torment of love and desire, aching to touch him, to stroke that hard powerful body, to kiss him and make him forget his grief as she knew she could.

There had always been that fierce primeval desire between them, drawing them inexorably together, flaring in anger, melting in passion, but for Jase it was not love. He loved Eva, had fathered her child.

Lexa's mind was spinning emptily, so crammed with thoughts she felt she would not sleep, and then the whisky combined with many restless nights began taking its toll and her eyelids drooped, her body finally relaxing. She turned her face into Jase's brown throat and finally slept.

She woke early the next morning after sleeping deeply, her body stretching languorously, suddenly stiffening as her hand came into contact with the rough warmth of Jase's thigh. Everything came back to her, the pictures rolling into her mind like a slow-motion film. Rex was dead, and she still couldn't quite believe it. It was as unreal as the fact that Jase was lying by her side.

She lifted her head and looked into his face. His strong jawline was shadowed with dark stubble, he was watching her with lazy brilliant eyes and he smiled. 'Hello.'

That made Lexa smile too, although her cheeks were tinged with hectic colour. 'Hello,' she replied very softly. His skin gleamed in the bright early morning light, his potent attraction making her mouth run dry, making her ache with desire.

'Thanks for letting me stay,' he said quietly.

'I'm glad you did. I needed someone too,' she admitted, not quite meeting his eye.

She was almost unaware of her actions, the impulse coming from deep within, something she could not fight, she saw her hand reaching out to touch his smooth shoulder, her fingers drifting over the warm skin to where short black hairs curled from his chest.

She felt the abrupt tautening of his body, heard the sharp intake of his breath, then suddenly his hand closed over hers, stopping her dazed exploration. 'No,' he said expressionlessly, though the eyes that met hers were shadowed, rough with torment. It was like having icy water flung in her face, and she came to her senses immediately, pulling her hand from under his, sick with shame at what she had done, what she had invited. Jase had made it very clear that he did not want her. What had she been trying to prove?

'Lexa, listen to me. . . .' he began gently.

'No! Please, Jase, don't say anything.' She felt too embarrassed. She could not bear to hear him talk about it.

She hurriedly slid out of bed. 'I'm going to make some coffee. Do you want some?'

Jase sat up, the bed covers falling from the solid muscle of his body. 'Lexa, we have to talk!' His voice was sharp with irritation.

She turned from the window where she was pulling open the lacy curtains. 'Can't you see I don't want to?'

she demanded fiercely. 'I don't want to talk about anything to do with you and me!'

She didn't want to be hurt any more. She knew only too well what Jase would say if they talked. He was going to marry Eva, there was no place in his life for Lexa; she did not need that spelled out to her. It was only too clear in her mind.

'How long are you going to keep on running? he queried coldly, angry now.

'To get away from you, I'd run for ever,' she said painfully.

'We both know that's not true.' His voice was mocking. 'I've only got to walk across this room to show you that you're lying. Whenever I touch you, you have no desire to get away from me.'

The truth of his words sickened her, she was sick of her own transparency. Jase, Zack, they could see through her as easily as if she was made of glass.

'That doesn't mean I like you very much.' All at once she was icily calm, reaching a sudden decision. It had to be a clean break for her and Jase, otherwise she would be hurt over and over again, whenever he drifted into her life. It was the only thing to do, born of a desperate need for self-protection, but even so, she flinched as the cold words fell from her mouth.

'Do you know what I'd really like? I'd like you to get dressed and go. I don't like being used, and I have got my own life to live. You're not part of it, you never will be, so please go.' She met his blank gaze without wincing, amazed at her own self-control, hardly recognising herself.

Jase moved from the bed, drawing her eyes as he came slowly towards her. Lexa stood perfectly still, her heart breaking, gasping with pain as he pulled her brutally against his body. He tangled a hand in her hair, pulling back her head.

'Do you really want me to go, Lexa?' he asked softly, his cool breath fanning her cheek. Before she could answer, his lips touched her exposed throat very tenderly, seconds before his mouth parted hers and he began kissing her savagely, arching her body to his so that she thought her spine would snap, tenderness gone. She closed her eyes beneath that bruising assault, fighting the sweet unbidden response that she could feel burning inside her despite his deliberate cruelty. She hated herself, moaning softly, deep in her throat, her lips moving beneath his, her hands creeping up around his neck, powerless to resist him.

But as soon as he felt her response, Jase raised his head and released her immediately. His eyes glittered with contempt.

'Perhaps you're right,' he muttered roughly. 'I'm beginning to think that you're just not worth it.'

'Please go,' she said through stiff bruised lips, broken with pain.

Jase unhurriedly pulled on his clothes and Lexa tried to drag her eyes away from his powerful rippling muscles and smooth tanned skin. He looked at her once, his expression guarded, still angry, then turned and left the flat.

Still standing by the bedroom window, Lexa watched him striding towards his car. Once inside, he lit a cigarette, smoking it slowly before the car roared into life, pulling away from the kerb at a screeching speed, and Lexa began to cry.

The funeral was grim, held in the pouring rain. Jase was frigidly polite and Lexa had the feeling whenever his golden eyes rested on her that he was looking right through her. They were strangers, which was how she had wanted it, she repeatedly had to remind herself.

Nick had flown back from America for the funeral and to Lexa's surprise, Eva was also there, standing between Nick and Jase. Marny came back to the flat with Lexa when it was all over. They drank tea and sat by the fire, the weather like a winter afternoon.

'Fancy Eva turning up,' Marny remarked, revealing that she had been as surprised as Lexa.

'Do you know her well?' Lexa did not know what prompted her to ask. Hadn't she put Jase out of her life once and for all?

'Not really. Nick was crazy about her, you know, he used to talk about her all the time, but I only met her half a dozen times at the most.'

'According to Nick, Jase stole her from him,' Lexa said flatly.

Marny raised her eyebrows in surprise. 'Really?' I can't believe it. Jase wouldn't do that, not when he knew how much Nick cared for her.' She paused, as though trying to recall something important. 'Oh yes, now I remember. Nick brought her home for the weekend, just before they split up. She was very impressed with Jase—well, you know the effect he has on women. I suppose she flirted with him and Nick was madly jealous. It's not really stealing, though, is it?'

Lexa shrugged. Obviously Marny didn't know about the child, and Lexa hadn't told her that Eva and Jase had been together in Nice.

'As far as I remember, Jase didn't seem at all interested in her,' said Marny, then lifted her hands in a graceful, puzzled gesture. 'Of course, Nick could never see straight when it came to Eva.'

'What about you?' Lexa asked, changing the subject. She was sick of going round in circles over Jase, although she found herself falling into it every single time. 'Are you still seeing Vic?'

To her surprise, Marny flushed, her eyes suddenly very bright and luminous. 'Actually, he's proposed,' she confided with a soft smile.

'Are you going to accept?'

Marny laughed. 'I already have.'

'Oh, Marny, I'm so happy for you!' Ridiculously Lexa felt tears filling her eyes. So Marny had finally got over Jase and fallen in love with someone else. Perhaps there's hope for me yet, she thought sadly.

'Thanks. I got tired of waiting for Jase,' Marny said half-jokingly, somehow reading Lexa's mind, reminding them both of her long-ago embarrassing confession in Lexa's bedroom. 'You haven't met Vic yet, have you?' Lexa shook her head.

Marny smiled. 'Perhaps you would come out for dinner with us some time this week. I'm dying for you to meet him. You'll like him, he's gorgeous!'

'I can't wait.' Lexa felt envious in the nicest possible way. She could see the love shining in Marny's eyes and knew that the older girl was going to be very happy, which was the very least she deserved.

One burningly hot afternoon a week later, Lexa returned home depressed, after an unsuccessful interview for a secretarial post, to find Eva Sutherland on the doorstep of her flat. Staring at her in surprise, Lexa approached the front door, wondering what on earth Eva was doing there. 'Are you waiting for me?' she asked with a polite smile, as she searched in her handbag for her key.

Eva nodded, a faint air of nervousness about her. 'I'd like a word with you, if that's all right.'

'Of course. Come in.' Lexa led the way, her puzzlement growing. She could not imagine what she and Eva had to talk about.

In the bright lounge, she flung down her bag on the

sofa. 'Sit down,' she smiled. 'Would you like some coffee?' Eva nodded, seating herself awkwardly in one of the cane chairs near the window.

When they both held cups of fresh coffee and the silence was building up, Lexa finally said. 'What did you want to talk to me about?'

Eva had hardly spoken a word since arriving and Lexa's curiosity was getting the better of her. She stared at the other girl, thinking, as always, how pretty she was, a sharp dart of jealousy lancing through her.

'Actually, I wanted to talk about Jase.' Eva's voice was quiet, tentative, and Lexa stiffened.

'Why should you want to talk to me about him?' she asked warily.

Eva stared into her coffee cup. 'I . . . I know it's none of my business—I don't even know if I'm doing the right thing coming here, but. . . .' There was a slight pause, then she blurted, 'Do you care for him?'

Lexa opened her mouth to speak and shut it again, her attention suddenly diverted by the ring she spotted sparkling on Eva's engagement finger. It was an emerald, large and flawless, set in platinum. 'You're engaged,' she said inanely, feeling as though she wanted to die. Jase had finally admitted his love to the world. It really was the end.

Eva smiled, brightness transforming her face into radiant beauty. 'Yes. I can hardly believe it myself, after all these years. We came so close to losing each other.' She paused, choosing her words carefully. 'In a way, that's why I came here today. I made a lot of mistakes, I needed help, and luckily Jase helped me. Without him Nick and I would never have worked it out, so you see I feel I owe Jase a big favour. . . .'

'Nick?' Lexa's mind was quicksand, her eyes wide and desperate. 'You're engaged to Nick?'

Eva nodded happily. 'Who else? There's never been anybody but Nick, there never could be, I think I knew that even when . . . well, when we split up.'

It was more than Lexa could take in. Eva was engaged to Nick! Where did that leave Jase? 'But Nick said . . .' she began confusedly.

'I know what Nick said—he told me. We were both so stupid.' Eva paused, then looked at Lexa determinedly. 'Look, Nick only told you half the story, I want to tell you the rest.'

'There's really no need. . . .'

'Oh yes, there is. It doesn't take a genius to see how you feel about Jase. Nick's given you totally the wrong impression, I realised that when he told me, so I'm here to straighten it out, once and for all. I was seventeen when I met Nick, and I fell for him almost immediately, but my parents were very strict, and when I say strict, I mean *strict*! They disapproved of Nick right from the start—he was too old, they said, he didn't have a respectable job, so I had to meet him secretly. We'd been seeing each other for a while when I discovered I was pregnant. You can imagine how I felt! I couldn't bring myself to tell my parents—I was petrified. And for some reason, I got it into my head that Nick would be just as angry if I told him. His career was just taking off, he didn't need the problems of being saddled with a wife and child. I also knew that my father would ruin Nick if he found out. I was too young, very confused, and very alone. I went to the house for a weekend around that time. It had been arranged weeks before and I didn't have a good enough excuse to back out. I'd already decided that the only thing to do was to break off with him.' She smiled self-deprecatingly.

'I was so noble and so silly. Of course the weekend was a disaster. I found myself flirting with Jase, who was taking absolutely no notice of me, in an effort to keep away from Nick. We rowed and rowed. Nick was convinced that it was Jase, that I'd fallen for him. I couldn't get rid of him, he kept on coming round to the house, and I was afraid that my father would kill him, when he found out about the baby, I knew I wasn't going to be able to hide it from my parents for very long. So I finally told Nick that it *was* Jase, that I was seeing him and didn't want to see Nick again.' She shrugged, seeing Lexa's look of astonishment. 'It was the most stupid thing I ever did. I didn't even think of the trouble it would cause. Anyway, I was so upset and confused that I also told Nick about the baby. I just wanted to get rid of him. Everything had gone terribly wrong and I knew it was over for us. I realise now that, for some insane reason, Nick thought the baby was Jase's. I might have mistakenly given him that impression, I can't remember. That afternoon was just a nightmare—Nick was jumping to conclusions faster than lightning, and I was letting him.

'Well, to cut a long story short, I went out to Nice to stay with Clea and Larry. I had to get away for a while, to sort myself out. I felt under pressure from all sides, my parents, Nick—I couldn't cope.' Her eyes dulled with sudden pain.

'I lost the baby—I fell down a flight of steps when I was sightseeing. It was the worst time I can remember, lying in that French hospital facing up to what a mess I'd made of my life. When I came out, one of Larry's friends got me a job in Monte Carlo, serving drinks in one of the casinos, and that's what I was doing until Jase found me, through a mutual acquaintance.

'He's been wonderful, he sorted it all out for us. He talked to Nick in America, he came to Nice to see me. He brought us both together again, and I don't know how we'll ever repay him. Coming here today was one thing I could do for him, and I wanted to explain things. He's very low at the moment, and I can't stand seeing him so miserable, so angry, he seems to be tearing himself to shreds inside. And from what I can see, you're just as miserable—so, to get to the point of my visit, won't you go and see him?' Eva finished pleadingly.

Lexa just sat there in silence, totally stunned by Eva's story, hardly able to believe her ears. It all made such perfect sense and she knew it was the truth. She was ashamed that all along the line she had believed Nick, had always doubted Jase. She cringed when she remembered the accusations she had flung at him, the cold way she had treated him.

'You were in his arms,' she remembered aloud. 'At the villa, the day of the party.'

Eva laughed. 'Jase had just told me that Nick was still in love with me. I couldn't believe it, I broke down. He was comforting me, that was all.'

A bubble of pure happiness burst inside Lexa. Jase hadn't been involved in any deceit, and she wanted to see him desperately, to apologise. She had been so blind.

'I . . . I don't know where he is. . . .' she faltered, very unsure of herself suddenly.

'He's at the house,' Eva told her with a smile. 'Do go and see him.'

'I don't know. . . .' Their whole relationship had been coloured by misunderstanding. Lexa had constantly turned away from him because she had thought him involved with Eva. And although she now knew that he never had been, that didn't automatically mean that there was a chance for her, it didn't mean that Jase cared.

But she did owe him an apology, a million apologies. She owed him the chance to reject her as she had rejected him. 'I'll think about it,' she promised at last, with a slight smile.

Eva got to her feet. 'He needs you, I'm sure of it.'

Lexa opened the front door. 'Thank you for coming, and thank you for explaining everything.' She was filled with gratitude and affection for this girl who she had been so nasty with, so jealous of.

Eva smiled. 'As I said, I owed it to Jase.'

'I hope I'm invited to the wedding.—congratulations, by the way,' Lexa added belatedly.

'Of course you are. I might even ask you to be a bridesmaid,' Eva threatened laughingly. 'I'll see you soon.'

'Yes—goodbye.' Lexa watched her go, not shutting the door until the other girl had disappeared round the corner. She walked slowly back into the lounge and sat down, her thoughts racing away, her need to see Jase again overpowering her as she made her decision.

She showered and dressed in a soft dress of patterned silk, made her face up carefully and brushed her hair until it shone, then left the flat and drove to the house, the muscles in her stomach knotting as the miles were eaten up. Twice she stopped, wanting to turn back, losing her courage, and she was actually shaking as she turned up the long drive.

Jase's car was parked outside the front door, and taking a deep breath, Lexa let herself into the house, her heart beating like thunder.

Twenty minutes of wandering through the house proved that Jase was not there and stretched her nerves to screaming point. She walked through the french windows, past the pool, finding herself walking towards the river and her favourite spot. She was planning what she would say to Jase; she wanted to get it right this time, and her head was bowed in thought. She strolled through the trees, stopping dead in her tracks as she saw him in front of her.

He was standing on the river bank, watching her approach. She stared back at him, still walking towards him. He was wearing old jeans that clung to his lean hips like a second skin and his chest was bare, the tanned skin gleaming like oiled teak in the hot sunlight.

As she finally stood in front of him, with only a few inches between them, she saw the lines of weariness in his face, the guarded expression in his eyes.

'What brings you here?' he asked coolly, neither of them bothering with greetings or particular politeness.

'I came to see you,' she whispered truthfully, her whole body rigid with nervousness, her heart pounding in her chest, deafening her.

'About what?' He stared at her, his eyes flicking over her expressionlessly.

Lexa's courage seemed to fail her again, all her carefully rehearsed words forgotten.

'The house seems empty without Rex,' she said quietly, prevaricating like mad. 'I kept expecting to see him coming——'

'Why have you come here, Lexa?' Jase cut in tersely, his powerful body as tense as hers.

She looked quickly up into his face, then her eyes dropped, resting on the buckle of his belt. She stared at the arrow of dark hair that disappeared beneath the belt, the muscled flatness of his stomach.

'Eva came to see me this afternoon. She . . . explained everything.'

'And?' Jase's voice was hard, uncompromising. He was not going to help her.

'Why didn't *you* tell me the truth, why did you let me think . . .?'

'Perhaps I wanted to break the crazy image you had of me,' he said flatly, casually, as though it didn't matter at all. Lexa closed her eyes. He did not care what she thought of him.

'Well, I . . . I came here to apologise for all those things I said to you. I was wrong and I'm very sorry,' she said quietly, and to her dismay, felt tears filling her eyes as the silence grew.

'I guess that makes us about even,' Jase said at last with a slight smile, accepting the apology.

Lexa's head jerked up, the tears spilling on to her cheeks. 'Yes, I suppose it does.'

'Don't cry,' he said gently, reaching out and flicking away the tears with his fingertips.

Again the silence built up. 'I . . . I'd better go,' she sniffed, feeling utterly miserable.

What had she hoped for anyway? Jase didn't say a word, just stared at her narrow-eyed. He did not ask her to stay and it seemed desolately obvious that he did not care for her. Eva had been wrong and Lexa had clutched too tightly at the other girl's words, feeding the tiny spark of hope that had persistently refused to die.

She blindly turned away and took a few steps towards the trees, then stopped dead and turned back, as Jase said, very softly. 'Just where do you think you're going?'

'Back to my flat,' she snapped, her nerves suddenly breaking. He was playing games with her. She supposed she deserved it, but that didn't make it any easier to bear.

'Still thinking of marrying Zack Harvey?' Incredibly, he was smiling.

'No, I'm not,' she replied flatly, her breath catching in her throat at the flaring warmth in his eyes.

'That's good, it saves me having to stop you,' he said softly.

'You ... you....' Lexa bit her lip savagely and began to walk away. Jase caught her before she had taken two steps, pulling her round to face him, smiling into her angry green eyes.

'Lexa, don't run away again,' he murmured, touching her face, trailing his long fingers across her heated tear-stained cheeks.

'Let me go, Jase.' She wriggled in his grasp, knowing how futile it was to try to fight his immense strength.

'Not a chance, my love. I'll never let you go again.'

Lexa forgot to struggle, staring into his golden eyes, her heart stopping at his huskily-spoken words. 'What do you mean?'

'Exactly what I say. I've waited too long for you, Lexa, and I can't wait any longer.' His hands caught her tightly against his hard body and his mouth touched hers, brushing her lips with aching slowness. 'I love you,' he muttered into her throat, his cool breath mingling erotically with hers. 'I'll always love you.'

'Jase!' She whispered his name, her heart bursting with pure sweet happiness. 'I love you too—so much. I've loved you since I was sixteen years old.'

She heard his shaken groan as his mouth parted hers, his muscular arms drawing her even closer to the bare warmth of his chest. He kissed her deeply, hungrily, until she was clinging to him weakly, her body soft and yielding against his. Then he slowly raised his black head and she gazed into the burning depths of his eyes and saw a love so strong, so fierce and all-encompassing that it made her heart twist painfully inside her.

'It's always been you, Lexa,' he admitted huskily. 'Always.'

'But ... But you didn't want my love when. ...'

He stopped her with his mouth, his tongue sensuously tracing the trembling responsive outline of her lips. 'Didn't I?' he asked wryly. 'I was burning up for you, aching to make you mine. I'd been thinking of you for two years, and the minute I heard you were coming home from Switzerland, I was on a plane over here.' He sighed, his arms tightening possessively, his eyes shadowed with pain. 'You were so beautiful. You took my breath away and I couldn't keep my hands off you. But you'd only just left school, you had no experience of life, of men. I wanted you—so badly, but how could I take you? You needed your freedom, needed to live a little and make up your mind. I was afraid that you'd grow to hate me if I tied you to me so young. I would have had you for a couple of years, maybe, when I wanted you for the rest of my life. I was out of my mind!'

'I could never hate you,' Lexa whispered against his warm bare shoulder, flicking his skin with her tongue, revelling in his instant response. She knew now why he had been so cruel in rejecting her.

'You had every reason to, I guess. You don't know what a temptation you were! When I caught Nick coming from your room, I couldn't control myself. I was as scared as hell that you'd fall in love with somebody else. It was sheer blinding jealously, that's why I was so cruel to you, so bloody unreasonable. I was even jealous of Zach Harvey, and knowing you believed that rubbish about Eva only made me more furious. I know I treated you badly, and I'm sorry. I'll make it up to you, I'll spend the rest of my life making it up to you '

Lexa smiled, her love shining in her emerald eyes. 'Did you think of me when you got back to New York?' she asked teasingly.

Jase laughed. 'Put it this way: I was hell to work with for that whole year. You were constantly on my mind. I nearly went insane, but I knew it was the only thing to do. I think Rex guessed how I felt, he rang me and told me you were going to Nice.'

Lexa's eyes widened in surprise. 'He knew?'

Jase nodded. 'And I think he approved. Anyway, I couldn't wait any longer, I needed to see you again, so I flew over. It was only by chance that I found out Eva was there. It was painfully obvious that she and Nick were both still in love, so I decided to play Cupid.'

'And it worked.'

'For them, yes, but I thought I'd blown it with you. I was convinced that you didn't give a damn about me any more, it was only the fact that you melted so sweetly whenever I touched you that gave me any hope. There was never anything at all between Eva and myself. I swear to you, I never touched her, I never wanted to.' He was actually pleading for her to believe him, and she touched his hard-boned face, needing to reassure him.

'I know that now—Eva told me this afternoon. Oh, Jase, I was so stupid! I loved you so much and I was so sure you didn't love me. I was afraid that you'd find out how I felt, that I'd make a terrible fool of myself, that's why I was so cold,' she explained regretfully, sad for all the time they had lost in misunderstanding.

'I'm so glad it's not too late,' Jase murmured against her white throat, his mouth warm and disturbingly sensual. 'Because I need you, Lexa, I need you with me night and day, for ever. Marry me, soon.'

'As soon as you like,' she accepted softly, her smile tempting as she slid her arms around his neck, stroking her fingers through the thickness of his hair.

Three weddings, she thought happily. Everything had

turned out fine for her and Jase, and Nick and Eva and Marny. Rex would have been so pleased, so very pleased.

'I love you so very much, Jase. Please don't leave me,' she begged softly.

'I'll never leave you.' He was kissing her mouth, brief hungry kisses that made her ache for more.

'Tell me you love me, show me that you do,' she whispered desperately. Their eyes met, Jase's flaring with hunger and love and raw need.

'I love you, Lexa,' he said deeply. 'Believe me, there's only you, and I can't live without you.'

He lifted her effortlessly into his arms and carried her back to the river bank, laying her gently on the soft grass, in her favourite secret place—his place too, as she had found him there.

He brought his powerful body down next to her, his mouth parting hers, his fingers moving, deftly unbuttoning her dress, searching for the satin warmth of her skin, as he began to make love to her.

Lexa responded with loving, trembling passion, knowing for certain that he loved her fiercely, that the rest of her life would be spent within the strong hungry circle of his arms, that she would never be alone again. There was nothing else in the world that she wanted.

Harlequin® Plus
FROM MODESTY TO NUDITY

Poor Lexa! Having taken off her bikini top to acquire an even tan, she hardly expected Jase to burst in on her privacy. Yet the sophisticated Jase was probably not at all shocked, for seminude sunbathing is quite commonplace, particularly in Europe. But this certainly has not always been the case.

Until World War I, women's beachwear usually included vast capes, turbans, flowing dresses, woolen leggings and lace-up boots. The accent was on modesty and soft elegance, not fitness and practicality, and women were clothed from head to toe.

By 1920, skirts, bloomers and sleeves became shorter, and some women began wearing "daring" one-piece swimsuits, sleeveless outfits that buttoned down the side and reached to the knee. Even so, wraparound dresses were worn over them, and were slipped off only at the water's edge.

In the twenties and thirties bathing suits gradually grew scantier, revealing more skin every year. The bold women of the mid-thirties were able to wear two-piece suits, which were so risqué that they exposed a few inches of skin at the waist!

Today, that suit might be referred to as an early "bikini," but the name didn't come along until July 5, 1946. At a Paris fashion show, designer Louis Reard presented his newest two-piece swimsuit, which he named the bikini, after an atoll in the South Pacific where the Americans had just tested an atomic bomb. Both the bomb and the bikini were, said Reard, "the ultimate."

Reard was to be proven wrong, however. For by the 1970s nude swimming and sunbathing became the rage of Europe, and now many countries all over the world have specially designated "nude" sections on their beaches.